Two Nights A Week

Tekla Series

Leigh Jarrett

Published by Steambath Press (self-published)

Paperback 1st edition published July 2012
ISBN-13: 978-1927553015
ISBN-10: 1927553016

Paperback 2nd edition published October 2017
ISBN-13: 978-1-927553-44-2

To my eldest son, who like Chad, shared so much of his life,
thoughts, and ponderances with his mom.
Your trust and openness is something
I will treasure forever.
You are deeply loved

Chapter One | Monday

The trees were only starting to turn color, but the wind was bringing in some icy cold arctic air. Chad Parker pulled his jacket closed as he made a run from his car to the front doors of Tekla Senior High School. It was already the second week of classes, but he'd only just transferred in from a school that was in the next city over. Tekla had a football academy that Chad and a few of his friends had decided to take advantage of when the program had been opened up to accept students from other school districts. He was running later than usual because he'd slept in, and his friends had made other arrangements for the first day, so he hadn't had them to rely on as his backup plan for waking up on time. It had taken him nearly forty minutes to reach the school even though he'd been traveling at top speed.

It was times like these that Chad hated living out as far as he did. But his father had insisted on it. His family owned a string of high-end hotels in the middle of Vancouver, but his father had wanted what he considered a more wholesome environment to settle his family in, so he'd built a massive estate almost five hours in from the west coast of Canada.

Chad was an only child, and they'd moved into the estate just after he'd turned eight. Luckily, there had been an elementary school close to his home, and he'd managed to make a lot of friends. He was good looking, naturally outgoing, and partially due to the amenities in his house, Chad had become very popular.

He checked the time on his phone as he opened the door into the school office and smiled at the secretary sitting behind the counter at her computer, but it didn't look like she was in the mood to be swayed by his charm.

"Can I help you?" she asked blandly.

"Yeah. Today is my first day," Chad replied. "I transferred here for the football academy, but I don't have a timetable yet."

"And you're late. Name please."

"Chad Parker."

"What grade are you in?"

"Twelve."

Chad looked around as he waited for the secretary to print off his timetable. The notice board contained very few items, but he perused the information anyway to pass the time. There was a stack of documents on the counter, and he lifted one. It had a map of the classroom locations on it, so he folded it up and stuffed it in his pocket. He was about to start reading through a newsletter when the secretary came back with a printed copy of his timetable. He thanked her and stepped out into the hallway.

His first class was History 12 in room 136 with Ms. Clare. He pulled the map out of his pocket and was relieved to see it was only a few doors away from where he was standing. He found the room and peered in the window of the door, spotting two of his friends sitting at the back of the room. He quietly opened the door and nodded his apology to the teacher as he made his way toward the back. He exchanged silent high fives and a few stupid faces with his friends before taking a seat in the only vacant spot in the room.

After falling into his seat, Chad placed his books on the table he'd be sharing with the guy next to him. Once he had himself organized with his binder and a pen, and the teacher went back to instructing the class, he turned to introduce himself.

"Hey, I'm Chad." Chad held out his hand under the table to avoid detection by the teacher, who was probably already annoyed at his disruption.

"Hi. Derek Steeple." Derek shook Chad's hand and then went back to taking notes from the board.

"Would I be able to borrow your notes for the last two weeks?" Chad asked as he pulled some paper out of his binder and began writing down the information the teacher had written on the board. He'd always been good at school, managing to maintain an average of about ninety-six percent in most of his classes, except French. Languages were not his thing, but Chad needed one to get into the university his father had picked out for him. History was one of his favorite classes, and he wanted to make sure he hadn't missed anything crucial in the two weeks he'd been absent.

He turned to face Derek, waiting to hear his response.

"Umm …sure," Derek agreed as he flipped through his binder and unclipped the rings to remove about twenty pages of notes. "It's pretty detailed, but you only need to know the definitions and the dates and stuff to pass the course."

"Thanks, buddy," Chad replied. "I'll photocopy these at break and give them back to you."

After an hour of tedious detail regarding the cause and effect of any potential world conflicts, the bell rang for break and Chad made a dash for the office before it became too crowded. His friends from his history class, Sam and Dillon, were waiting for him when he emerged from the office.

Sam and Dillon had been friends with Chad since grade two, and the three of them were practically inseparable. Their elementary school teachers had always referred to them as the *Three Musketeers*, and they'd continued their close friendship all the way through high school. But of the two of them, Chad considered Sam to be his best friend.

"Why were you so fucking late?" Sam asked as he began pushing buttons on the vending machine they were standing next to in an attempt to coerce it to drop a bit of change.

"We were starting to think you'd changed your mind about coming to Tekla," Dillon added. "You had us worried."

"I wouldn't leave you guys without your best quarterback," Chad replied. "Why didn't you phone me if you were so worried?"

"We did. Your phone is off …again," Dillon said, then jostled Sam out of the way, as the machine began dispensing free bags of chips.

"Fuck, are you kidding!" Chad fished his phone out of his pocket and turned it on. There were ten missed calls and a stack of text messages waiting. He swore as the bell for the start of class rang. "Damn, I have to piss. Can you give these papers back to the guy sitting next to me? I'll be there in a minute."

"You're seriously going to tick that teacher off," Sam said then waved the papers away, not wanting them, as he continued to stuff bags of chips into his jacket. "You better get moving."

"I know. I'll be quick. Just give the guy next to me his notes and put mine under my binder." Chad pushed the stack of paper at Dillon and took off down the hallway, in what he hoped was the correct direction to find the washrooms.

He finally found them and relieved himself quickly, but decided to check his appearance before he headed back to class. He had dark blond hair, which he wore short, and had startling blue eyes that were common in his family. He stood about six feet tall and had his dad's rugged good looks, which had provided him with an obsessive following of girls wherever he went. He'd decided to wear the football jacket from his previous school today over an old t-shirt and jeans and was pleased to see his friends had decided to do the same. They needed to stick together until they met a few people and felt more comfortable with their new school.

Chad headed back to class and peered in through the window of the door at the back of the classroom, which turned out to be locked, so he motioned for Dillon to let him in. Dillon reluctantly pulled himself out of his seat and opened the door.

The teacher didn't look impressed as Chad took his seat.

"I'm sorry, Ms. Clare," Chad said. "But as you know I was running late this morning ...and I'd had three cups of coffee before I left the house ...I was dying for a piss." A few people laughed aloud, and Ms. Clare cleared her throat. "And then I had to photocopy the notes for the past two weeks of class because I aim to get an 'A' this semester. I love History. It really is my favorite subject—"

"Thank you, Mr. Parker," Ms. Clare interrupted. "I look forward to seeing your enthusiasm reflected in your first assignment."

Chad opened his binder and stuffed the photocopied notes into it before taking out the papers he'd been writing on earlier so he could take down the new information that was on the board.

"Did I miss anything else?" Chad showed Derek what he'd written down so far.

"There's a test Wednesday on chapter one through five," Derek replied, so quietly Chad almost missed what he'd said.

"Fuck, I don't even have a textbook yet," Chad said. "This is shaping up to be the week from hell for me."

"You could borrow mine. I already know this stuff."

"That would be fantastic. Thanks, buddy." Chad clapped Derek on the back and then leaned into the aisle to attract Sam's attention.

"Do we have a practice today?" he asked Sam.

"No, just a meeting. Fifteen minutes tops," Sam answered.

"Do you need a ride home?"

"Yeah, we'll catch a ride with you." Sam sat up and pretended to be working as Ms. Clare made her way down the aisle.

"Mr. Parker," Ms. Clare said. "You might think you're pretty hot shit coming into this school as a star quarterback, but I will not be putting up with any more of your interruptions."

"I'm sorry," Chad replied. "I'm feeling so overwhelmed by everything. I don't normally behave like this ...I promise." He smiled confidently at the teacher until she sighed and made her way back to the front of the class. It wasn't long until the bell rang and Chad found himself back out in the hall trying to locate his next classroom before he took off for lunch. He was on his own for now, because Sam and Dillon had been called to the office to complete their registration.

"What do you have after lunch?" Derek motioned for Chad to hand him his timetable. "Physics 12 with Mr. Peters ...impressive. That's near my locker. I'll show you the way. It's a bit tricky to find because you have to go in behind the gym." He handed Chad the history textbook and started walking toward the gym. "So, you transferred in with those other guys?"

"Yeah, there are five of us from my old school. Tekla has an excellent football academy. Are you into football?"

"I watch it with my dad sometimes." Derek stopped in front of his locker and deftly spun the dial around until he had it unlocked. "Your physics class is just across the hall there."

"Yeah. Hey, thanks for the textbook," Chad replied. "Maybe I'll see you around tomorrow." He punched Derek in the arm and headed across the hall. A group of boys was standing outside the classroom talking. They were all wearing Tekla football jackets.

The largest guy of the group stepped forward.

"Hey, you're one of the new guys, right?" he asked.

"Yeah," Chad answered. "Name's Chad …quarterback. Are you in this physics class?"

"Unfortunately," replied the ominous, obvious leader of the group. "Mr. Peters is a real douche. He says I've gotten behind on some of my labs, so I have to spend lunch in here catching up.

"That sucks."

"Yeah. Hey, my name's Zeek, and this is Marlboro and Pete."

The other two just nodded.

"Cool," Chad replied. "So, how come there's no practice today?"

"With all you new guys coming in, they had to reshuffle things a bit. There'll be a full practice tomorrow." Zeek moved closer to Chad so he could speak quieter. "Just a head's up. You do *not* want to be seen talking to that freak, Derek."

"Why not? He seems all right." Chad looked back to see that Derek was still at his locker trying to fit everything back in, but books kept spilling out onto the floor and being kicked away from him down the hallway. He was a bit of a lightweight in comparison to most other boys their age, and he was dressed a lot nicer than any of them as well. Chad watched as Derek struggled to close his locker door, but was thwarted when a random passerby hauled the door open causing the contents to spill back onto the floor.

Chad sighed and turned away, and followed Zeek into the physics room to see if he could find out what he'd missed.

The football meeting turned out to be nothing more than an opportunity to introduce the new players and have them sized up for their gear. The entire thing still managed to take forever, and forty-five minutes had passed before they were finished and heading to the parking lot. It had started to rain at the beginning of the meeting, but now it was bucketing down, and they had to make a run for the sleek new sports car Chad's parents had bought him for his eighteenth birthday.

He unlocked the doors and climbed in, but had to wait while Sam cleared a bunch of beer cans and hamburger wrappers off the passenger seat before starting it up. He'd already been in trouble more than once at his old school for firing up his stereo while the doors were still open.

Chad let Sam fiddle with the stereo while he backed out of the stall, and was about to floor it out of the parking lot when he saw Derek standing in the rain, without even a coat on. He wheeled around so Derek would be on the driver's side and rolled down his window, then reached over and turned the stereo down, fanning the air out of the car as Dillon lit up a joint in the backseat.

"What are you still doing here?" Chad asked Derek.

"I'm waiting for my ride, but I don't think he's coming."

"Who? Your dad?" Chad brushed his thumb across his bottom lip as he watched Derek. "Did you try calling him?"

"Yeah. No. I don't have a phone."

"Here, you can borrow mine." Chad reached into his jacket, pulled out his phone, and handed it to Derek, then turned around to Dillon, grabbed the joint, and took a long drag before handing it back. He brushed his hand over his jeans. "Fuck," Chad whispered under his breath. The rain was splashing in through the open window, soaking his clothes, so he began fiddling with the heat as he waited for Derek to complete his call; he didn't appear to be having any success. Chad rolled the window up a bit.

Sam's phone beeped, signaling a text message, and he instantly started howling and pounding the dash before turning in his seat to show Dillon what was coming up on the screen.

"Oh my god," Sam continued, laughing as Dillon began grunting and moaning in mock ecstasy.

"Hey, Dillon. Watch it back there, would you?" Chad shouted as he looked over his shoulder at Dillon. "Don't be jacking off in my backseat, or I'll make you fucking lick it up." He threw a lighter at Dillon and just shook his head as the guys critiqued what turned out to be nude photos of some girl on their new cheerleading squad.

"He's not answering," Derek said as he moved timidly toward the car and handed Chad his phone back.

"Where do you live? I'll give you a lift." Chad opened his door and jumped out, then pulled his seat forward and pushed at Dillon with his foot to get him to move over.

"Put it away, Dillon," he warned. "I'm fucking serious."

"That's all right," Derek said, backing away. "He'll probably show up eventually."

"By which time you'll have drowned," Chad replied. "You're not even wearing a coat. Come on, they won't bite, I promise."

When Derek hesitated, Chad leaned back into his car, and Derek could hear Sam complaining as he climbed through the center of the car and into the backseat.

"There you can have the front seat," Chad said. "Much less scary, unless of course, you're afraid of crazy ass driving habits." Then he slid into the driver's seat, reached across, and popped open the passenger door, motioning for Derek to get in.

Reluctantly, Derek circled the car and got in, making sure his seatbelt was done up before setting his bag down on the pile of beer cans at his feet. He cringed as Chad reached over and turned the volume of the stereo back up and yelled at him to tell him his address. Derek contemplated yelling back, but then decided to write his address on a piece of paper, and handed it to Chad, who immediately typed it into his GPS system. He'd never been in a car with as much power as what was about to be wielded, and it made his heart jump in his chest as Chad revved it up.

Chad, wanting to relieve some of the stress of the first day back, burned a few doughnuts in the parking lot before peeling out into the street. He reached back and took the joint from Dillon again, flicking at it before taking a drag. He almost dropped it as he fishtailed around a corner and took off down one of the side streets. With the car back under control, Chad extended his arm, nudging Derek on the shoulder to take the joint off him.

"No, thank you." Derek shook his head, but Chad wasn't paying any attention to him; he was trying to read his GPS while changing the track on the stereo. He took the joint from Chad and turned around to pass it to one of the guys in the back seat. Sam grabbed it from him and yelled something that he couldn't make out at all. It became clear when Sam passed him his phone and pulled up one of the pictures they'd been looking at.

Derek knew the girl in the photo. She was on the cheerleading squad, and he'd known her since kindergarten. He couldn't understand why the girls thought it was a good idea to take naked photos of themselves and send them to the football players. It was asking for trouble, in his opinion, but then maybe that's what they were looking for. He smiled and nodded at Sam as he passed the phone back, and then pointed out his house to Chad.

Derek stood on his front step, watching as Chad reversed at top speed out of his driveway, and flew off into the traffic. He pulled his key out of his bag and let himself into what he knew would be an empty house. His parents were both working most evenings that week, but his dad was supposed to have driven him home from school before he went to work. As usual, he'd forgotten.

Soaked through, Derek grabbed a towel to dry off with and flicked on the television before heading to the kitchen to forage in the fridge for anything halfway edible. He found a loaf of bread and some cheese to make a grilled cheese sandwich, but before he could start cooking, he had to dig in the sink for a frying pan and wash off what was probably food from days ago. As it was cooking, Derek pulled a milk jug out of the fridge and took the cap off to smell it. Totally off ...typical, he thought, almost choking as he walked over to the sink to pour it out.

Derek had been taking care of himself for as long as he could remember. His parents had always worked two or more jobs each, and he was often alone in the house until well past midnight. He didn't mind it so much. At least it was quiet when his parents weren't home. When they were home, it was like living in a war zone, the screaming and launching of projectiles being a constant occurrence. When he was home alone, he could sit in peace and watch television in the living room instead of having to hide out in his bedroom. He wasn't always at home in the evenings though. He had a part-time job at the local mall in one of the exclusive clothing stores where he worked two nights a week plus Saturdays. It provided him with an excuse to be out of the house, and enough money to fund his ever-increasing wardrobe. He had a lot of fun with his clothes, experimenting with lots of different styles, even though it tended to draw a lot of negative attention from the other kids at school. Not that he cared.

He flicked the television off and headed back to the kitchen. And after surveying the area, he decided to wash up the dishes and clean all the rotten food out of the fridge before heading off to his room to study for Wednesday's history test, from what few notes he had. He still couldn't believe he'd lent his history textbook to Chad like that. It was rare for someone like Chad to speak to him, never mind actually be civil. It had thrown him off. He'd spent most of his high school years as a bit of a loner with the occasional friend that was usually worse off than he was. Eventually, those friends always ended up transferring to a different school to avoid the bullying that was rampant at Tekla. He'd managed to survive by keeping a relatively low profile, avoiding places like the cafeteria and the gym. He exhaled an exasperated sigh and flopped down on his bed to start studying and doing his homework.

Chad flipped through the history textbook and took his own notes on the chapters they were having the test on. He'd been a bit late getting started because the weed they'd been smoking after school was a bit stronger than their usual stuff, and he'd passed out after dinner. His mom had woken him up at nine to ask him if he had any homework to do, and he'd reluctantly pulled himself out of bed and headed to the office that was part of his bedroom suite. He'd been at it for two hours and was about to pack it in when his mom showed up at his door with a cup of herbal tea for him.

"How was your first day?" she asked as she threw some blankets aside and took a seat on the sofa across from his desk.

"I was really late," Chad replied. "And I pissed off my history teacher. But other than that, it was all good."

Chad's mom shook her head, *tsking* under her breath.

"Did you meet the other boys on your football team?" she asked.

"Yeah, we had a kind of meet and greet thing after school today. They seem like decent enough guys. We'll see how they stack up tomorrow at practice."

"Any new friends yet?"

"I gave a guy from my history class a ride home today. He lent me his textbook to study from. We have a big test on Wednesday."

"Didn't he need it?"

"No, he told me he knew everything already. He seems pretty cool. But some of the guys from the team told me to stay away from him." Chad leaned back in his chair and blew across the top of his tea to cool it off before taking a sip. "Mom, why is it that people are so freaked out by anyone that's different?"

Chad's mom wrinkled her nose in thought.

"Anthropologically speaking," she replied, "it's a survival mechanism. But in today's society, it's unnecessary and socially irresponsible."

"Yeah, but you're forgetting how ignorant the common teenager is. Which is why I dress the way I do, instead of like Derek."

"Is Derek the boy from your history class?"

"Yeah, he's into all the designer labels, and stuff …you'd love him." Chad drained his teacup and stood to give his mom a kiss. "I'm going to bed. I'm spent, and I have practice after school tomorrow, and I don't want to be playing *cream the new guy*."

"Chad, please be careful," she said as she studied her son with concern. "We'll see you in the morning for breakfast. I think the cook is planning on making your favorite waffles."

She ruffled her son's hair on her way out the door and stopped to lean against the wall after she closed it behind her. The idea of Chad starting at another public school for his final year of high school had seemed insane to her after everything he'd been through at his old school.

If it had been entirely up to her, she would've sent him away to a private school instead, where he'd be safe. At least he wasn't at Tekla alone. He had his football friends from his old school to protect him if he got himself into trouble again.

Chapter Two | Tuesday

Chad pulled the timetable from his pocket and looked it over. It was a different system for the classes than he was used to. He only had four subjects to deal with each semester, but each class was almost three hours long, and it alternated from day to day. It was going to take a bit of time to get used to, but after locating the proper block, Chad was pleased to see it was English; another of his favorite classes. He climbed the stairs, assuming that any classroom starting with *two* would be on the second floor.

Looking around, Chad didn't see any of his friends in the class, but at the back sat Derek—alone. Chad took an empty seat a few rows up from where he was sitting. The last thing he needed to do was piss off the guys on his team by sitting with the guy. It was a sure fire way to get himself injured during practice. He was pleased that he'd made that decision when he saw Marlboro and Pete wander into the room and take a seat at the back, across the aisle from Derek.

Chad pulled a piece of paper from his binder and wrote *Hey Fuckwads* across it, then crumpled it up and chucked it at them. They howled with laughter as they read it and tossed an eraser at his head. He had just lifted the eraser from the floor, about to throw it back at them, when the teacher arrived.

"Excuse me, Mister ...," the teacher said.

"Parker, sir. Sorry." Chad turned back in his seat and opened his binder while trying to look as abashed as possible.

"Right," the teacher began. "Today we're going to be reading *A Rose for Emily* by William Faulkner. He was a writer from the southern states during a time of great change ..."

Chad tried to pay attention, but he was finding the content of the poem to be so dull and irrelevant that he was having trouble staying awake. When a question sheet was handed out, he cringed but set to work completing it.

"This is horrible stuff, isn't it?" the girl next to him commented as she leaned in his direction, touching his arm.

"I hate these kinds of poems," Chad replied. "Why not just write a short story instead of trying to sell the thing as a poem."

"Totally. My name is Ivy," Ivy said, batting her eyes.

Chad let out an inner sigh but smiled.

"So, how are you managing so far?" Ivy asked, and then poised herself to hang on Chad's every word.

"It only being your second day and all," she added.

"I'm doing all right," Chad answered. "I'm Chad by the way."

"Yes. I know. You're a quarterback aren't you?" Ivy replied. "I'm on the cheerleading squad." She shifted her chair closer and leaned into Chad's shoulder, lowering her voice to an intimate whisper as if she were about to tell him a secret. "We're having a start of season party at Zeek's on Friday. Did you want to go?"

"Sure, yeah." Chad nodded his head. "That sounds cool."

"Great. Here's my address."

Ivy tore a small piece of paper from her binder and wrote down her address and cell number. "You can pick me up at eight."

Chad bit his lip and then grinned.

"Nice. Here's my number …just in case you need me …for anything. Anything at all." Chad winked at Ivy, then took her hand and used his pen to write his cell number on her arm. He knew from experience that girls like Ivy craved the bragging rights that came with having a football player's number written on their arm.

And he was only too willing to oblige.

He'd just finished when the bell rang for break.

Ivy bounced up out of her seat, and took off into the hallway, probably off to find her squad to show them the number. Chad decided to stay in the classroom for the break to work through the poem in front of him. He was about to get started when Marlboro and Pete attacked him from behind, putting him in a headlock and playfully roughing up his hair.

"You lucky bastard," Pete said. "Did Ivy give you her number?"

"Yeah," Chad replied, grinning. "Apparently, I'm taking her to Zeek's on Friday night."

"You're only here two days, and you already get to tap something like that." Marlboro dropped himself into the chair beside Chad and threw his feet up on the desk. "I'm so fucking jealous."

"Hey, what time does practice usually finish on a Friday?" Chad asked. "I want to make sure I have enough time to swing by the drugstore and replenish my glove box before picking Ivy up."

He smiled as the guys started howling and pounding him on the back. They were so fucking predictable—it made him sick.

"Are you going out for break?" Pete asked.

"No," replied Chad. "I want to get this stupid worksheet done in class, so I don't have to work on it tonight. I have to study for a history test."

"All right, see you later," Marlboro said. "Hey, by the way, watch your back. The freak is still in the room. You don't want him sneaking up *behind* you. If you know what I mean."

Chad forced a smile and a nod in Marlboro's direction, keeping it fixed in place until the two left the room and headed outside.

He pressed the worksheet flat on his desk, smoothing out the wrinkles caused by his eraser. Anything to delay wading through the next question. He could hear Derek's pencil scratching away behind him. Other than that, the silence was deafening, leaving Marlboro's comment to churn around inside his head.

Chad turned in his chair to face Derek. "I'm sorry about that," he said to Derek. "Those guys are complete assholes."

"I'm used to it," replied Derek. "It's not a big deal. But thanks."

"I don't understand what is wrong with some people." Chad left his seat and went to sit beside Derek. "It's like someone forgot to turn their brains on when they were born." He leaned forward on the desk and paused for a moment "Hey, thanks again for the notes and the textbook. I finished my own notes last night. Did you need the textbook back? I have it in my locker."

"Just bring it to class tomorrow." Derek shuffled nervously as the bell rang, signaling the end of the break. "You should get back to your seat before anyone sees you sitting back here with me."

"Yeah, right. I'll see you tomorrow."

Chad squeezed Derek's shoulder affectionately as he passed by, making Derek jump, then slid back into his seat, imagining the flush of heat that was likely coloring Derek's cheeks.

The rest of the class crept by painfully slow, and Chad was relieved when the bell finally rang, and he could go find his friends. The plan was to meet up and throw a football around during lunch. He found Sam and Dillon out in the furthest field with a joint already lit as they passed the ball back and forth. He intercepted a pass and howled as Sam nailed him into the ground, knocking the breath clean out of him.

"Hey, fuckers!" yelled the other two guys from Chad's old school as they ran onto the field and took off after Dillon, trying to grab the joint from him. The bigger of the two was Gus, short for Augustus, which they never let him forget. And the other guy Tyler was new to their group. He'd only been hanging out with them since tenth grade, but Chad trusted him implicitly. He'd proven his loyalty on more than one occasion.

Rain began spitting down, slicking up the grass, so they decided to take shelter under a tree to wait it out.

"So, party at Zeek's on Friday. Are we going?" Gus asked, then stuffed an entire sandwich into his mouth and laughed, almost choking on it as Tyler punched him in the ribs.

"Yeah, I have to go," Chad said. "I got myself roped into it by this girl, Ivy, in my English class."

"Fucking typical," Tyler said, leaning forward and pulling out tufts of grass in irritation. "Why do they always go for you?"

"Oh my god! She's the one in those pictures!" Sam shoved Dillon and scrambled to pull his phone out of his pocket. He brought up the pictures before passing his phone around.

"That is so fucking unfair," Gus said as he perused the pictures and shook his head. "What the hell are you going to do with her? She looks like she'll be looking for a little action."

"My usual," Chad replied. "Get her so drunk she passes out then spread some lascivious rumors around school about our night together and hope she doesn't remember that I didn't touch her."

"What a fucking waste," Dillon said.

"Anyway," Chad said. "Enough about my girl problems. My house on Sunday to watch the game?" Finishing his apple, he tried to see how far he could chuck it across the field. Dillon snorted out a laugh as it careened into a nearby tree.

"As always. We'll be there," Sam replied. "Are we still coming over tomorrow to watch a movie or something?"

"Sure, if you want," Chad replied. "But my mom will be home, so we have to stay off the smut channels. Your choice if you still want to show up."

"As long as you've got beer, we'll be there," Gus said, then laughed loudly, snorting. "Hey, I made a rhyme."

"That doesn't fucking rhyme, you moron," Dillon said, grinning. "How did you manage to get through elementary school?"

Gus' forehead wrinkled in thought.

"What do you mean?" he asked, then squealed as Dillon tackled him and pushed his face into the ground, before leaping up and taking off at top speed back toward the school.

Chapter Three | Wednesday

Chad slid into his seat just as the bell rang, prompting a round of applause from his friends to celebrate his lack of tardiness that morning. He fished around in his backpack, pulled the history textbook out, and set it on the table, pushing it over toward Derek.

"Thanks again, man," Chad said as he tried to make eye contact with Derek. "I would've been dead without it." Then he stood and looked around the room, not spotting the teacher anywhere.

"Sure," he said. "I'm here on time today, and where is our valiant Ms. Clare? Nowhere to be found."

He hooted loudly as the other students laughed with him, then sat back down, the show complete. He propped his head on his hand and faced Derek. "So, how was your night?"

"Boring," replied Derek. "I had to work last night."

"Yeah, where do you work?"

"At the mall. In a clothing store."

"Cool. I went straight home and crashed in my room." Chad turned in his chair, redirecting his attention on Sam. "Who did you buy that shit from yesterday? If I'd wanted to take a nap, I would've stolen some of my mom's sleeping pills."

"Hey, we're still new here," Sam replied, clearly offended. "I'll track down a good supplier. Give me some time to talk to a few people, go to a few parties. You know."

"Yeah, yeah, sure." Chad turned back to Derek. "Who do you buy your stuff from?"

"I don't. I'm not really into all that." Derek slid the textbook closer to himself and flipped it open to one of the chapters they were about to be tested on—if the teacher ever showed up.

"Good for you." Chad leaned closer and bumped Derek's arm with his hand before he lowered his voice slightly. "I owe you for the textbook. What are you doing for lunch?"

Derek picked at the edges of the paper in the textbook.

"I don't usually eat lunch," he answered.

"No wonder you're so thin. I saw a sushi place a few blocks from here." Chad winked at Derek. "Let me buy you lunch."

Derek tucked the textbook closer to his chest, hugging it to him.

"I don't know," he said.

"Derek, you can't get fat eating sushi. Those couture jeans of yours will still fit tomorrow, I promise." Chad smiled then leaned heavier into his hand so he could study Derek's face. He hadn't noticed the small amount of makeup Derek wore around his eyes before. It was subtle. Just a bit of mascara and black eyeliner, but it gave Derek's already expressive eyes an exotic touch.

"Should I meet you out front of the school?" Derek asked, then blinked, breaking Chad's gaze.

"No, I'll pick you up at your locker. My car is parked around back today in the covered lot."

Chad was about to ask Derek something else when he felt a pencil hit the back of his head. He redirected his attention to find that Ms. Clare had arrived, and was standing at the front of the class with another pencil in her hand at the ready.

"I'm sorry to interrupt, Mr. Parker," Ms. Clare said. "But the rest of the class would like to start the test."

Chad turned to face the front of the room and sat quietly while the tests were handed back, and set to work immediately, finishing in less than half the allotted time. He returned to his seat after handing the test in and watched Derek slowly, but correctly, completing the questions.

As the bell rung for break, Chad closed his books and nudged Derek with his knee before getting up and following his friends, Sam and Dillon, out the door. They jostled their way down the hall together, kicking each other and pushing people into lockers until they arrived at the washroom.

"Chad, we're going to throw a ball around at lunch again today," Sam said. "Meet us on the far field. We'll save you a spot on the wet grass with a little dry grass of our own."

Amused at himself, Sam laughed and pounded Chad's back.

"Sorry, I can't today," Chad said. "I'm taking Derek for sushi."

Both his friends fell silent.

"Damn it, Chad," Sam said finally and grabbed Chad's shirt, pulling him across the room away from the flow of guys coming and going from the washroom.

"What are you doing?" he asked.

"Nothing." Chad pushed Sam's hands away. "It's all good."

"Your rules, remember. No one from school," Dillon said. "This is only our third day, and you're ignoring your own rules already?"

"It's not a fucking date, asshole," Chad said to Dillon, and then directed his attention on Sam. "He lent me his textbook. Plus he's too fucking skinny. Give me a break, would you?" He pushed Dillon out of his way and stepped around Sam before turning to face them. "I appreciate that you guys look out for me, really, I do. But I can take care of myself sometimes, all right?"

"Fine, Romeo," Sam replied. "But make sure your cell phone is on for a change, in case we have to locate your body at the bottom of the lake." He smacked Chad in the back of the head on his way past and followed Dillon out into the hall.

The bell had rung over fifteen minutes ago, and the halls had cleared out as people found their way to the cafeteria. Chad had taken off right after class to *deal with some stuff*, and Derek had been left standing and waiting at his locker.

Derek decided he'd waited long enough, and subjected himself to enough ridicule by passing students for one day, so he opened his locker to grab one of his binders and a few books to head to the library, as he did every day at lunch.

Chad was coming back from the parking lot where he'd frantically cleaned the crap out of his car and was now running down the hall toward Derek's locker. He saw Derek crouched down rooting around at the bottom of it, and slowed himself down so he could sneak up on him. He positioned himself directly behind the open locker door and knocked lightly on it.

It didn't quite have the desired effect.

"You're late," Derek said, slamming the locker shut.

Chad scrubbed a hand around to the back of his neck.

"Yeah. Hey, I'm sorry. Are you ready to go?"

"Will we have enough time?" Derek asked as he followed Chad out through the side door that led to the covered parking lot.

"That's the nice thing about sushi," Chad said as he opened the passenger door, motioning for Derek to climb in. "It's usually pretty quick."

Derek nodded as Chad closed his door then twisted in his seat, peering around, amazed at how tidy the car was compared to the state it had been in before. He carefully did up his seatbelt as Chad slipped in beside him, preparing himself for the deafening music and squealing tires—but none of that happened.

"How do you think you did on the history test?" Chad asked as he turned the engine over and slowly backed out of the stall, before heading toward the street.

"I think I did all right," replied Derek. "What about you?"

"I got a couple wrong. But I'll get an *A* like you."

"How do you know what my mark is going to be?"

"I was watching you after I handed mine in."

Chad glanced over when there was no response. Derek appeared to be deep in thought, picking nervously at the crease of his pants.

He checked the rear-view and pulled into the parking lot of a small strip mall a few blocks from the school. He turned off the engine and pocketed the keys.

"Just stay there," Chad said. "Wait for me."

Derek tracked Chad as he climbed out of the car and closed his door. He undid his seatbelt and looked over his shoulder as Chad came around to the passenger side to open his door for him, making him extremely uncomfortable. But while they were waiting to be seated in the restaurant, Chad chatted away about football and his old school, and the uneasy feeling went away—until Chad placed his hand at the small of his back as they were being led to their table, making him jump—yet again.

"So, what are you going to have?" Chad asked.

"I've never had sushi before," Derek admitted as he turned the menu over, trying to figure out what, if anything, he'd be able, or willing, to eat. "I'm not really sure what …"

Chad patted the table, smiling as he caught Derek's attention.

"Then let's stick to something without raw fish," he said as he waved the server over, and much to Derek's relief ordered for them both. The yam rolls Chad had ordered sounded safe enough.

"So, where do you live?" Derek asked as he refolded his napkin and glanced around the restaurant, noting it was practically empty at this time of day, except for a few business people.

When Chad didn't answer, Derek looked up to see that Chad was studying him intently. "Chad?"

"We're up in the estates on *Hillside*," Chad replied finally.

"Wow! Are you rich or something?" Derek laughed and squeezed a lemon into the water the server had just dropped off.

"Or something." Chad leaned back in his seat and crossed his arms. "Derek, I'm having trouble figuring you out."

Derek released the lemon, allowing it to sink to the bottom of his glass. "What do you mean?"

"I'm getting all sorts of mixed signals from you."

"What kind of signals?" Derek examined the plates of food as they were set on the table. He cringed as he realized the only utensils they were going to be getting were chopsticks.

"The clothes, the makeup, and the mannerisms tell me one thing," Chad replied. "But then I try to touch you, and you jump."

Derek, having just taken a sip of water, began coughing into his napkin, his mind raging, furious, as he looked at the stereotypical teenaged, football jock in ripped jeans and a baseball cap sitting across from him.

"All right, jokes over," Derek said. "This wouldn't be the first time one of you jocks has tried to make a fool of me. I'm not that stupid. And we're going to be late getting back to school." He threw his napkin down on the table and made to push his chair out when Chad reached across the table and grabbed his arm.

"Whoa, Derek," Chad said. "I'm not joking around. I was being perfectly serious." He slid his hand down Derek's arm and grabbed onto his hand, squeezing it. "Believe me, I'm the last person that would try to make fun of you." He let go of Derek's hand and reached for his chopsticks, clicking them together.

"Now, have you ever used these things before?" he asked.

"Never."

"Here, watch." Chad showed Derek how to hold the chopsticks to carefully maneuver the sushi into the soy sauce, and then into his mouth. He tried not to laugh as Derek dropped a piece, spraying soy sauce all over the white tablecloth.

"You just need to practice some more," Chad said. "I'll have to bring you here every week until you become a pro."

Derek set his chopsticks down and leaned against the table.

"What are you doing?" he asked. "Why did you bring me here?"

"Honestly," Chad replied. "You seem like a really nice guy ...and you've got the most amazing eyes."

"My eyes? You're definitely fucking with me." Derek leaned back, heavily, and crossed his arms. "Guys like you do not go around telling guys like me that you like our eyes."

Chad shrugged.

"Yeah, you're right," he said. "Because, as I was sitting here, watching you eat, I suddenly realized it's your mouth that's driving me crazy."

Derek clenched his jaw then spoke, his voice dropping to a harsh whisper. "You're a fucking idiot, you know that? We're late. And I don't want to play your little game anymore."

He motioned to the server and spoke quickly to her. "Could we get separate checks, please? And could you call me a taxi?"

"Wait. No. Just ignore him," Chad interjected. "One check, please." He waited until the server left before reaching out to grab Derek's hand again. He had to grip on to it tightly to keep Derek from pulling away. "You've got me all wrong. I'm not pulling your chain, honestly." He relaxed his hold.

"Why don't I believe you?" Derek pulled his hand away and crossed his arms. "Do you have any idea how many times I've been screwed with over the years? Guys like you. You don't have a clue what it feels like to be tormented and made fun of—because you're usually the ones doing it. So, don't tell me I *have you all wrong*. I know exactly who you are."

Chad shook his head.

"I'm sorry people have hurt you in the past, but I'm not one of them," he said. "If anything I'm completely on your side."

"And how do you figure that?"

"The reason I transferred to Tekla wasn't just because of the football academy." Chad pulled his chair in tight against the table and leaned as far across it as he could. "Someone secretly videotaped me over the summer, and when school started in September, the tape showed up on the football coach's desk—as well as a few people's cell phones. Everyone found out about it, and I was politely asked to leave the team."

"So what?" Derek said. "Someone videotaped you."

"The video …it was of my boyfriend and me—and we were …you know. Someone had hidden a camera in my parents' boathouse where we used to go sometimes for a bit of privacy. When the football coach saw it, he freaked."

"You had a boyfriend?" Derek screwed up his face in disbelief and laughed sharply. "Now I know you're fucking with me."

"Derek. Stereotype much?" Chad answered. "Just because I like playing football and I dress like a jock, suddenly I can't have a boyfriend?"

"All right, for argument's sake, you had a boyfriend. Was he one of the guys on your team?"

"Yeah. But worse than that, my boyfriend was the coach's son."

"Ouch."

"You're telling me. I've never seen anyone turn that many shades of purple in my life. My parents tried to smooth things over with him, but in the end, we decided it would be better for me to change schools. So here I am."

"How did you manage to get your friends to transfer with you?"

"We've all been friends since we were like eight, except Tyler. He didn't start hanging with us until high school. But my other friends ...they've known I was gay since like sixth grade, and they've always had my back. They didn't want me heading over here on my own."

"They sound like great friends."

"They're the best," Chad replied. "They've taken a lot of slack and more than a few punches in the face because of me over the years."

Derek relaxed into a seat, uncrossing his arms.

"What about your parents?" he asked.

"Same. I told my parents I thought I liked guys better than girls in sixth grade. They held out on complete acceptance until I was in grade ten though. Now, they're cool with it."

Derek's features softened, and he dropped his voice.

"My parents don't have a clue," he said.

"That's rough. Why haven't you told them?"

Derek sighed heavily. "Long story."

"Tell you what. I have all the guys coming to my place on Sunday to watch the game. Why don't you come over? They'll fill you in on all the gory details of being my protectors."

"Yeah right," Derek said. "I've just confirmed I'm gay and you invite me to a house full of football players."

Chad dropped his hand on the table and laughed.

"You're really paranoid, aren't you?" he said.

Chad paid the check, then reached out and squeezed Derek's hand again before getting up from the table. "Sam and Dillon are coming to my place after practice tonight for dinner. It's just the two of them. Why don't you come too? My mom will be there."

Derek still looked suspicious.

"Fine," Chad said. "Give me a second." He pulled his phone from his pocket and dialed a number as they stepped outside. "Hey, Mom. Yeah …why? Did they phone already? We're not even that late. I know …I know …Mom …Mom. I've invited that guy I like from school over tonight. Yes …I know …sure. Anyway. I'm trying to convince him that I'm not setting him up …yes, I know. Could you talk to him? Yeah, all right …thanks."

Chad held out the phone and Derek took it and held it to his ear.

"Hello?" Derek said timidly, not sure what to expect.

"Hi, Derek. This is Mrs. Parker. Chad's mom."

"Um …nice to meet you?" Derek crunched up his face at the fact she'd known his name already.

"There's no reason to be concerned about Chad and his friends. They're all lovely boys, and it'll be nice to meet you. Chad hasn't stopped talking about you since his first day."

Silence.

"Derek, are you still there?" she asked.

"Yes, I'm here. Sorry. I guess I'll see you tonight then."

Derek handed the phone back to Chad and waited until he'd finished speaking with his mom before following Chad over to the car. He stepped back as Chad opened the car door for him, shivering as Chad ran his hand down his arm. He climbed into his seat, and his heart felt as though it was thudding out of his chest as Chad slid into the driver's seat and closed his door.

"We're really late," Chad said. "It's already one thirty. We could go back to school and face the wrath of our teachers for being late, or we could hang out at your place until I go to practice."

"Is there a third option?" Derek asked.

"Sure," Chad replied. "We could go to the beach just down the road from here and hang out."

Derek shook his head, no.

"It's freezing down there," he said.

"So, we'll stay in the car and watch the gulls getting thrown around by the wind. Come on. We can talk some more. Get to know each other."

"We could do that right here without having to drive anywhere."

"But there are so many cars coming and going …" Chad leaned back into his seat and watched Derek. "And that is exactly why you want to stay here." He slid his hand into Derek's and turned sideways in his seat. "You really can trust me."

"I'd like to. Really, I would. But I have to be careful."

Chad studied Derek's face, allowing his gaze to wander over Derek's delicate features. Too much. He let go of Derek's hand and turned to face his steering wheel, gripping it tightly in both hands.

"Fuck," Chad whispered under his breath. "You are so fucking hot. It's killing me." He turned back to face Derek. "Is it all right if I kiss you?"

"Maybe," Derek replied. "But do you mind taking your hat off? I can't stand baseball caps, or what they do to a guy's hair."

Cold air rushed in, and Derek shrieked, covering his mouth with his hands in amusement, as Chad rolled down his window and chucked the baseball cap out through it.

"Done," Chad said.

"You didn't have to do that," Derek said, laughing.

"You will never see me wearing one of those ever again," Chad replied. "I promise." He took the keys out of the ignition, threw them up on the dash and turned back to face Derek.

"Well, that's much better anyway," Derek said as he ran his fingers through Chad's hair, trying to fix up what the hat had done to it. He was just smoothing out some of the tendrils around the back of Chad's neck when Chad reached for him.

"Can I kiss you now?" Chad brought his forehead to rest on Derek's and watched the movement of Derek's eyes as he stared back at him in amazement. "Because I'm having trouble breathing …I want to kiss you so bad."

"I don't know." Derek dropped his gaze and sighed to himself. His heart hammered away in his chest as he thought about the likelihood that Chad was making up all the stuff they'd talked about, and that his mom had somehow been messing with him as well; it was all too unlikely. He shifted himself closer to Chad and cradled Chad's face in his hands.

"Is that a *yes*?" Chad lowered his head, then looked back up into Derek's face with a softness that had Derek dismissing any doubts he was having. As soon as Chad saw Derek nod his head in agreement, he ran his hands up into Derek's hair and pulled him in. He took Derek's mouth tenderly, not wanting to scare him, but as Derek responded with increasing urgency, Chad slipped his tongue into the warmth while his hands started a quest to bring Derek closer to him. He was about to climb over to the passenger side to recline the seat and take more of what he was craving from Derek when someone knocked on the driver's side window.

"You've got to be fucking kidding me." Chad sat up and cleared a small patch in the opaque, steamed up window to look out through.

"Who is it?" Derek asked anxiously.

"It's Zeek and his pack of goons." Chad turned the power on in the car and rolled his window down a crack. "What the fuck do you want, Zeek? I'm trying to get busy in here."

"I can see that," Zeek answered roughly. "Who have you got in there creating all that heat?"

"None of your business, jackass. I don't kiss and tell." Chad moved his head to block Zeek's line of sight as Zeek shifted over slightly. "What the fuck do you want?"

"We saw your car sitting here all steamed up, and we thought we'd come over and check it out. Maybe see if there was any extra to go around. You'd share with us, wouldn't you?"

Chad peered out at Zeek, attempting to read him.

He was serious.

"Listen, Zeek," Chad said. "Ordinarily, I'm a generous guy. Ask any of my friends. But this one is really special if you know what I mean, and I don't want to share. On my honor, the next drunk skank I hook up with will have your name written all over her."

"All right," Zeek replied, nodding. "Just this once, because you're new. But that's not how we do things around here."

"Got it. See you later." Chad rolled the window up and turned to face Derek, who was visibly shaken "I wasn't going to let him see you." He reached for Derek to comfort him. "Are you all right?"

"How can you carry on a conversation like that so casually?"

"Practice," Chad replied. "I've been hiding who I am for a long time from idiots like that." He looked back over his shoulder as he heard someone knocking again. "Now what?" He cracked the window a bit and looked out. "What do you want, Marlboro?"

"Your hat was blowing away out here," Marlboro replied. "I chased it down for you. Open your window so I can pass it in."

"Nice try," Chad said. "I don't want the hat. It's a piece of crap."

"Are you kidding me? These things sell for like two hundred and fifty bucks, maybe more."

"Then you keep it."

"Thanks, man." Marlboro pulled the hat on and leaned easily against the car. "Hey, I was just talking to Sarah, and she says she saw you leave the school with that freak, Derek."

"Who's Sarah?"

"My girlfriend. Where the hell have you been?"

"On a planet where fuckwads like you don't have girlfriends."

"Hah. Hah. So, what's up with Derek?"

"He felt sick, so I gave him a ride home."

"Chad, buddy. Zeek specifically told you to stay away from him. He's a fucking queer you know."

"Really? Duly warned, my friend." Chad looked up and realized that the fog effect was beginning to clear from his window. "I have to go. I'm starting to lose my cover." He reached over and motioned for Derek to duck down out of sight.

"Hey, just between us," Marlboro said. "Who have you got in there with you?"

"Someone amazing who is off limits to you Neanderthals," answered Chad. "Now get away from my car, or I'll run over your fucking feet. I'm out of here. See you at practice."

Chad turned the car over, put it in reverse, and pulled out of the parking lot, headed in the direction of the school. Once they were a safe distance away, Derek pulled himself back up and looked out the back window.

Chad reached out for Derek's leg and gripped onto it firmly, brushing it with his thumb. "Are you all right?"

"That was the most freaked out I have ever been in my entire life. Those guys are seriously scary. You have no idea."

"Don't worry about them," replied Chad. "I've dealt with their type before." He looked over at Derek and smiled. "Hey, do you mind hanging out at the school while I practice, or do you want to go home, and I'll pick you up later?"

"You better take me home. I'm supposedly sick remember."

"Oh right. Good thinking. I'll pick you up at six?"

"Sounds good."

Derek wasn't sure what he should be wearing to hang out with Chad and his friends. Chad had mentioned they'd probably be watching a movie and ordering pizza, so he slipped on one of his older pairs of jeans and a sweater from last year's haute couture collection that he was planning to use as pajamas this winter.

When he heard Chad's car in the driveway, Derek raced down the stairs and went to slip on some old canvas loafers.

He sighed and stuffed his bare feet into the shoes, and hoped nobody would notice his toenails. They were still painted pink from the last time he'd worn flip-flops to work. Grabbing his coat, he flew out to the car before Chad had a chance to come to the door and see the squalor he lived in.

They drove for a good hour before Chad finally turned into the gated community that was *Hillside*. Derek's mouth dropped open as they turned on to Chad's driveway. He couldn't believe the size of the estate they were approaching and began wondering if the driveway was ever going to end. As they approached the house, he was speechless; the massive structure was like something out of the medieval ages. He still must've been staring open-mouthed as they took the last bend because Chad commented.

"My dad has a thing for castles and anything medieval," Chad said. "It's totally modern inside though."

"That is unfucking believable," Derek replied. "So, this is what "or something" looks like."

As Chad pulled up in front of the house, a man came rushing down the steps and opened Derek's door for him while Chad stepped around the car and handed off his keys to another man that drove the car away to park it.

Chad grabbed onto Derek's hand and led him up the steps to the front door that appeared to open of its own accord.

"Mom! I'm home!"

"I'm coming …wait," announced the intent of the beautiful, slender woman with long, blonde hair as she came out from one of the rooms off the front foyer. Derek recognized her immediately.

"You must be Derek," she said. "I'm Evelyn Parker. Chad's mom. It's so nice to meet you. My goodness, you look exactly as Chad described you, right down to those beautiful curls and gorgeous eyes."

"Oh, um ...," Derek stammered.

"Mom, please," Chad said. "You'll embarrass him." He nudged Derek affectionately and gripped his hand tighter. "We're going to hang out downstairs. Send the guys down when they get here."

"All right, dear." Evelyn patted Chad on the cheek before returning to the room from which she'd emerged.

"It's down this way." Chad took Derek's coat and handed it off to a woman, along with his own, and led Derek across the marble floor to a broad set of stairs leading into the lower level.

"My entertainment space is down here," he said. "There's a theater, lounge, a bar with an assortment of pop ..." He grinned. "Unless you look at the back of the cupboard, where I've hidden the good stuff. Then there's a bowling alley. And a pool that starts indoors, but opens up to the outdoors in the summer."

"And that's all for you?" Derek asked in amazement.

"What can I say," Chad replied. "My mommy loves me." He hugged Derek to him as they continued down the stairs. "Oh and there's an ice cream parlor from when I was younger. I don't use it, but it's kept fully stocked if you're into that."

"No, I'm not much into ice cream."

They reached the bottom step, and Derek cringed as Chad flipped his shoes into a closet, and reluctantly did the same. He could see why they needed to take their shoes off. The entire lounge and beyond was done up with a light cream carpet.

"Why on earth would anyone put such a light colored carpet in a kid's entertainment area?" Derek asked, mystified by the impracticality of the carpet choice.

"My mom is insane when it comes to decorating," Chad replied. "She's had to replace this carpet like five times already. My suite is down here as well." He led Derek through a set of double doors into a small living room with its own television, library, and gas fireplace. "My bedroom is off there with a bathroom attached and I have an office over there for doing homework."

"It's really nice," Derek said. "I wish I had this much space."

"Did you want to see what's on the television?" Chad asked. "We can go back out into the lounge. There's a bigger screen out there, and it's 3D."

"Yeah, sure."

Chad led the way and directed Derek to a spot in the back corner of a massive, L-shaped sofa.

"Do you want a Coke or something?" he asked.

"Sure, whatever you have. Coke is fine."

Chad moved through the bar and crossed the room with two cans in hand, stepped up onto the sofa, and walked across it to where Derek was sitting. He handed Derek one of the cans and scooted him forward with his foot, so he could sit behind him.

Derek felt a little self-conscious as Chad sat down behind him and stretched his legs out on either side.

"What do you want to watch?" Chad asked as he flicked through the channels. He stopped on a comedy channel.

"Keep it there," Derek answered. "This comedian is hilarious. I watched him on a different show a few nights ago."

"Cool." Chad set his can down on a table behind him and motioned for Derek to hand him his. "Now, where were we before we were so rudely interrupted this afternoon?"

Chad wrapped his arms around Derek and tipped him back against his shoulder, so he could take his mouth. His breathing changed as he pulled Derek tighter to him, wanting, needing more.

Derek stopped him.

"That's definitely where we were at this afternoon," Derek said as he looked up into Chad's eyes.

"My stomach has knots in it again," he added.

"Maybe I can work those out for you later. I know just the thing to get rid of them. It works every time. But if not, we could try again, and again, and again, until we get it right."

Derek dropped his gaze.

"Chad," he said. "I've only known you a couple of days. I'm not looking to get that serious. Not yet, anyway."

Chad shrugged.

"All right," he said. "I'll wait. I'm a patient person." He grinned. "Tomorrow maybe?"

"Very funny."

"I can't help it if you turn me on." Chad motioned for Derek to move over, then guided him down onto the sofa, and climbed on top of him. "What am I going to do with you?"

"Nothing, remember." Derek smiled as he saw the glint in Chad's eyes and sighed in exhilaration when he felt the full weight of Chad's body lower down onto him.

He readily took Chad's mouth.

"Jeez, Chad," Dillon said as he leaped into the room. "Get a room, would you?" He chucked a bag of chips at Chad's head, flopped down on the sofa next to them, and tapped Derek on the head.

"Hey, Derek," he said. "How's it going?"

"Um …fine?" Derek replied from beneath Chad.

Sam jumped down the stairs and had the same reaction as Dillon when he saw the two of them layered on the sofa. "You just couldn't keep your hands off him, could you? Man, I love you, but you are such a fucking waste of an outrageous male libido." Ducking behind the bar, Sam squatted down and rooted around in the fridge until he found the beer he was looking for.

"All right, we'll give it a rest." Chad climbed back to the corner of the sofa and grabbed his Coke. He took a long swallow and motioned to Derek. "Are you coming back here with me?"

"In a minute," Derek said. "Where's your bathroom?"

"Just down the hall there." Chad pointed off down the hallway.

After finding the bathroom, Derek stepped up to the sink to splash some cold water on his face and examined himself in the mirror. He was a good five eight and had jet-black hair that hung down in soft curls around his face. His eyes were a soft brown with long, thick lashes that he'd recently begun accentuating with liner and mascara.

Derek knew his features and stature were overly delicate for a guy, but he liked the way everything came together in an appealing package. He was proud of the fact he'd been attractive enough to land a job at one of the exclusive clothiers and had been particularly thrilled when he found out staff got forty-five percent off everything in the store, including the shoes.

Looking down at his pink toenails, Derek chastised himself for not thinking to put socks on. He checked out the flush in his face again and threw some more cold water at it. In all the years since he'd come out to himself, he'd never had a boyfriend, or even kissed anyone for that matter, and he was finding Chad's casual attitude toward affection a bit unnerving—and extremely exciting at the same time. He examined his eyeliner to make sure the water hadn't caused it to smear and then headed back to the lounge.

"The guys have picked out some mindlessly crude comedy," Chad said as Derek climbed back into his spot. "If you don't want to watch it, we can find something else to do."

"No, I'm good." Derek snuggled in against Chad's chest and smiled as he felt Chad's arms wrap around him, holding him tight. He sighed, content, as Chad kissed the back of his neck, imagining what it would be like to be Chad's boyfriend.

Crack-thud-crack

A series of knocks and bangs at one of the windows behind them had everyone jumping.

Chad swore under his breath when he saw it was Zeek and Pete, and realized they'd seen him holding Derek.

"Fucking nosy bastards," Chad said. "They just couldn't leave it alone." He scrunched his face up as he tried to decipher the stream of obscenities being thrown through the window. "They must've followed me after I picked you up."

He held Derek tighter to comfort him; Derek was shaking.

"What should we do?" Dillon asked while standing at the window with his middle finger up.

"Close the curtains and ignore them," Chad replied. "We'll deal with them tomorrow. Actually, Sam, could you call one of the security guards for me?" He lay a gentle kiss on Derek's head and gave the finger to Zeek and Pete through the window while Dillon closed the curtains. "Hey, I think I hear Gus and Tyler." He looked toward the stairs. "I thought they weren't coming tonight?"

"Did you mention anything to them about Derek?" Sam asked.

"Do you actually think they'll be surprised?" Dillon replied. "Our boy here is unstoppable, you know that."

"Ignore them," Chad whispered to Derek. "They just like to harass me." He tightened his hold on Derek and nibbled lightly at his ear. "I've only ever had two boyfriends." He lifted his head and raised his voice. "They're just jealous because I have a hot date with a cheerleader on Friday night and they don't." He ducked as Dillon chucked a cushion at his head.

"Which reminds me." Chad smirked mischievously. "I have to make a condom run on Friday after practice. One can't be too careful with a girl like that." He shrieked as Sam dumped the remainder of his beer over his head.

"Sounds like the party has started without us," Gus shouted as he burst into the room and headed straight for the bar.

He looked up as Chad and Derek climbed off the sofa, shaking the beer off their clothes.

"Who's your friend, Chad?" Gus asked.

Tyler pushed Gus out of the way and started putting more beer in the fridge and setting glasses in the freezer.

"This is Derek," Chad replied. "He's in two of my classes."

"Hey, Derek." Both Gus and Tyler waved at Derek, then opened up Tyler's backpack and began throwing a collection of pipes and bags of weed up onto the counter.

"And those two highly focused euphoria seeking jerks are Gus and Tyler," Chad said to Derek, then pulled away, propelling himself across the room.

"Hey, forget it guys," he yelled, then stormed behind the bar and started throwing a bunch of stuff back into Tyler's backpack. "The weed is fine, but you can't bring that other crap into my house, you know that. My dad would flip shit if he found out."

Chad shook his head and ran his hands through his hair.

"Sorry about that," he said to Derek.

"No, it's fine."

Derek fingered the edge of his sweater.

"Chad, I'm going to try and dry my sweater off," he said as he started heading back toward the bathroom, but Chad caught up to redirect him.

"Let me lend you something," Chad said, "or you're going to be soaked for the rest of the night." He slipped his arm around Derek's shoulders. "I think I might have a sweater just like that." He led Derek into his suite and into the bedroom where he pulled some clothes away from his closet door and flicked on the light.

Derek stood awestruck at the immensity of the space Chad had strictly for his clothes. He walked along one of the rows, running his hand over some of the textures, wondering when Chad would ever wear clothes as gorgeous as this. He'd only ever seen him wearing old jeans and t-shirts. He began flicking up the labels on some of the items and had to remember, consciously, to breathe.

"My mom buys most of my clothes for me," Chad said. "She keeps hoping I'll actually wear some of this stuff. But I keep telling her that if I were to wear this stuff to school, she'd have to come identify me in the morgue."

"This is like, my dream closet. I'd wear this stuff regardless."

"Then let's pick out some stuff for you ...for keeps. The clothes on this side are from a few years back, so there should be something that fits you." He paused, considering.

"You're not super fussy about the fashion *year* are you?" Chad asked as he flipped through the clothes he was referring to. "Most of these shirts have a fairly classic design."

"I'm speechless, Chad," Derek replied. "Are you sure?"

"Absolutely."

Derek approached the rack of clothing and started perusing through it. "I'll just grab a sweater for now, but I'll definitely take you up on your offer." Preoccupied with the choices, he shivered when Chad stepped up behind him and lifted the soiled sweater over his head, removing it. He could feel Chad's hot breath whisper down his neck and across his shoulders.

"We'll take this one off first," Chad said, then threw the sweater onto the ground, and ran his hands down Derek's torso to his hips. "I love the way you curve in, just here, above your hips. You've got such a hot little body." He pulled Derek to him and placed a row of gentle kisses across the back of his shoulders.

"I want to run my mouth over every bit of you," he said, "and use my tongue to drive you crazy." And to emphasize it, Chad licked a line up the center of Derek's neck.

"Chad ...," Derek whispered as he fought to recapture his runaway breath. "Please, no. Not yet." He sighed with relief as Chad backed away from him, then lifted a sweater off one of the shelves, noting it was from the same company as the one he'd just discarded and slipped it on over his head. He turned to talk to Chad, but immediately averted his gaze. Chad had taken the brunt of the beer, requiring a complete change of clothes ...which he was in the process of doing.

Derek lifted his gaze, audacious, and watched as Chad rooted through one of his drawers looking for a clean pair of underwear. He swallowed hard as the muscles of Chad's toned, naked body moved to pull the new pair on.

"Do you ever get the feeling you're being watched?" Chad asked. "I love that feeling. It makes me so hot." He turned around, smiling and laughing, and crossed the room to pull a pair of well-worn jeans off the rack to put on.

He hauled Derek into his arms and kissed him.

"Pick me out a shirt," Chad said. "I'll wear whatever you want. It could even match your toenails if that's your thing. My mom says I look good in pink."

"I was hoping no one would notice." Derek blushed and pulled away from Chad. "I did them up for work the other day."

"I think they're adorable," Chad replied, then flipped through the shirts and pulled a pink one off the rack. "I'm willing to put myself out there for you in solidarity."

"I could put on a pair of socks instead."

Chad's relief was palpable.

"That is a brilliant idea," he said. "Can I grab a white shirt instead then?"

"Yeah …that one over there with the pearl buttons."

Derek smiled as Chad made a production of putting the shirt on. He looked incredible in it. Sexy and sophisticated. So much better than the casual, football-jock attire. Derek smoothed out the material on the shoulders and did up the buttons for Chad before grabbing a pair of socks for himself.

"Hey, the other guys are staying here tonight," Chad said. "Did you want to stay overnight as well? I'm sure I could find somewhere warm and cozy for you to sleep."

"Chad—"

"I'll do my best to behave myself, I promise." Chad held up his hand in mock oath. "You can raid my closet in the morning, and I'll even make an effort to be on time for school."

Derek shook his head.

"I really don't feel comfortable with that," he said.

Chad's face dropped, and he stuffed his hands in his pockets.

"All right, I'll give you a lift home after the movie," he replied.

Derek couldn't help but notice that for the rest of the evening, Chad wasn't as affectionate, and he hoped he hadn't upset him to the point where Chad didn't want to see him anymore. No. He immediately corrected himself. If that's all it took to put Chad Parker off, then he wasn't interested in him after all.

The ride home in the car was silent and awkward, and Chad didn't bother to get out and open his door for him.

There were some mumbled, "See you laters," then Derek let himself into the house, ran up to his room, where he slammed the door and threw himself down on his bed. He was wiping away a few tears from his face when he heard a soft knock on his door; he hadn't noticed that his mom was home.

"Derek, where were you tonight?" she asked.

"At a friend's house watching a movie."

"Who drove you home?"

"The friend, Mom."

"That's a fancy car he's driving. Is he from around here?"

"No, Mom. He lives all the way out in *Hillside*."

"Oh, my goodness."

"Just forget about it, all right?" Derek wrapped a blanket around his body and pulled his pillow over his head. "We're not friends anymore anyway."

"I'm sorry. Well …goodnight."

The door shut. His mom was headed back downstairs to finish watching her program.

Chapter Four | Thursday

Derek was having second thoughts about going to English class. Zeek and Pete had definitely seen him and Chad together the night before, and he was sure the group of them had spent the rest of the night scheming up ways to punish him.

He'd gone to the office before class and spoken with the vice principal to alert him to the possibility that there might be trouble in the class. He always found that pre-warning the faculty was the best way to thwart any possible threats before things got out of hand. He was pleased when he saw his English teacher heading toward the office after being called over the intercom.

Slipping through the back door, Derek kept his head down as he moved to get past Marlboro and Pete who were doing their best to trip him up. He finally made it to his seat and braced himself for the onslaught of insults, but they were surprisingly quiet.

He peered over his shoulder and saw Pete pounding his fist into his hand while staring at him menacingly. They weren't going to be satisfied with simple humiliation this time. He was going to be in for a beating, he could see it in their eyes.

Derek tried to brush the tears from his cheeks as the teacher returned to the room and started sorting through some papers, but found that he couldn't stop the steady flow from falling onto his books. He would be safe during class, but as soon as the first break came around, he wouldn't be able to escape them.

"Hey, Derek. What's wrong?" Chad slipped into the seat next to him and gently brushed some of the hair away from Derek's face.

"What are you doing back here?" Derek pushed Chad's hand away and turned his back to him.

"Well, I was hoping to sit beside this guy I really like."

Chad glared over his shoulder when Marlboro and Pete started making stupid kissing noises.

"You totally blew me off last night," Derek said.

"Yeah, I'm sorry." Chad leaned in closer. "Derek, do you like me? Because that's the thing that kept going through my mind last night. I kept thinking maybe I'd been too pushy and you were too polite to say you didn't like me."

"No, Chad." Derek turned to face him. "I really like you."

A whispered, "Faggots," cut through the silence of the room.

"Shut the fuck up!" Chad jumped up out of his chair, knocking it to the ground as he spun on Marlboro and grabbed him by the front of his shirt. "This is none of your fucking business!"

"Mr. Parker!" Mr. White jumped out of his seat and set his stance with his fists on his hips.

"I'm sorry, Mr. White," Chad responded. "I was trying to have a private conversation with Derek …and Marvin here insisted on making an ass of himself." He gripped Marlboro's shirt tighter in his hands and gave him a shake before letting go, dropping Marlboro into his seat. "As if naming yourself after a cigarette doesn't make you look stupid enough."

Marlboro grunted and crossed his arms, slouching into his seat.

"Chad, please take your seat up here with Ivy," Mr. White said. "And for my sake, refrain from any more outbursts until class is over."

"I'm going to sit back here from now on." Chad opened his backpack and threw his books down on the table.

"Suit yourself. But I don't want any more trouble." Mr. White cleared his throat. "Today we are going to be watching a film about the civil war in the United States and how it affected the people in the south." He called up the movie on his laptop and turned on the smart board at the front of the classroom. "Marvin Dyck, could you switch the lights off?" A wave of snickering erupted across the room as Marlboro reluctantly reached over and flicked the switch.

Once the movie was well underway, Chad shifted his chair closer to Derek's and reached out for his hand under the table. As Derek's hand entered his grasp, he squeezed it tightly.

"I thought you ditched me because I wouldn't sleep with you," Derek said as he edged himself closer to Chad.

"I'm sorry I gave you that impression. I tripped over my vanity big time last night. It won't happen again."

Derek laughed quietly. "That has got to be one of the strangest expressions I've ever heard."

"My mom is always accusing me of it. It's one of my big shortfalls. My life has been blessed so far, and sometimes, I forget that not everyone is pliable or gullible enough to bend to my every fanciful whim and desire."

Derek snorted out a laugh.

"You're fucking hilarious," he said. "Who taught you to speak?"

"My darling mommy dearest." Chad laughed as Derek gripped his hand tighter and nudged him with his shoulder.

"Boys, please just watch the movie," Mr. White whispered as he leaned down to the height of their table. "There's only so much I can do to protect you if these two morons behind you decide to have a go at you."

"Thanks, Mr. White." Chad checked over his shoulder and watched as Pete made intimidating gestures at him. Luckily, they had a game tonight instead of a practice, meaning there shouldn't be an opportunity for anyone to injure him on the field.

At least he hoped that was the case.

He sneered back at Pete, flipped him the finger under the table, and went back to watching the movie.

The bell rang, and the lights went up as Marlboro switched them back on. Mr. White sat down behind his desk and set his cell phone in front of him in case he needed to call the school's police liaison officer. He seemed content to see if the boys could work things out between themselves for now, rather than involving the office.

Ivy gathered up her things and worked her way down the aisle to stand in front of Chad.

"Our date on Friday," she said. "Rescinded. You fucking queer."

"Oh, my poor heart." Chad slipped from his chair and fell to the floor, twisting around before playing dead. His eyes snapped open. "You wouldn't have been able to keep up with me anyway, bitch." He pulled himself back up and turned to face Marlboro and Pete. "And what do you two gits have to say about it?"

"You are so fucking dead," Pete said.

"Funny, I feel perfectly healthy."

"And what about your girlfriend?" Marlboro said, pointing to Derek. "How healthy do you think he'll feel after we finish with him?"

"Don't you dare touch him." Chad leaped to his feet and grabbed Marlboro, forcing him up against the wall. "You lay one finger on him, and you will pay dearly. Do you understand what I'm saying?"

"Oh, I'm so scared," replied Malboro, sneering. "The faggot is going to use his little fairy wings to beat me silly."

Pete snorted in amusement.

"Laugh all you want," Chad said, "but do you have any idea who my father is?"

"Who the fuck cares?"

"You and your family will care very much if you fuck with me." Chad pushed Marlboro hard against the wall and then released him. "Carl Lester Parker. Look him up on the internet before you threaten Derek and me again."

"Fucking freaks, the both of you!" Pete grabbed Marlboro and pulled him from the room with him.

"What was that about your dad?" Derek tugged on Chad's sleeve and pulled him back into the seat beside him.

"My dad is well connected …plus he says I'm his golden boy." Chad stretched out and shook off the tension that had been building in his shoulders. "I'm fucking untouchable."

Derek rolled his eyes.

"Chad, your vanity is showing again," he said. "Don't trip on it."

"That's a good one. I like that." Chad cradled Derek's chin and kissed him before pulling his chair even closer.

Mr. White cleared his throat.

"Sorry, Mr. White," Chad said, "but he's so damn precious, I had to kiss him."

"Just keep your hands where I can see them." Mr. White sighed and opened up his laptop and typed *Carl Lester Parker* into the search engine. He read through a few pages before looking up at Chad from beneath raised eyebrows. His student's threat had not been idle. Far from it. He averted his eyes, closed his browser, and started marking some papers for the next period instead.

"Are you coming to the game tonight?" Chad looked up to the front of the room to see if Mr. White was paying any attention to them, then ran his hands up Derek's thighs.

"I have to work," Derek replied.

"What time do you finish?" Chad tucked his hands around behind Derek's ass and dragged him and his chair closer.

He released Derek when Mr. White coughed in warning.

"I'm usually out of there by nine," Derek replied.

"Can I pick you up? We'll go for coffee or something."

"Sure. Do you know what store it is?"

"With those labels of yours," Chad replied. "I'm guessing it must be the place my mother considers to be her second home. I'm surprised you haven't seen her in there before."

"I've seen her. Briefly. When your mother wants to shop, we have to close the store and call in the senior wardrobe consultant."

"That sounds like her. She's a bit of an attention seeker."

"She does it very well." Derek kissed Chad quickly on the cheek and turned his chair back around when the bell rang.

The rest of the class passed without incident from Marlboro and Pete, which concerned Chad. He decided he was going to escort Derek to his next class after lunch and not let him out of his sight for the rest of the day. He'd have to drive him home as well to make sure he got there safely, which would make him late for warm up, but he wasn't going to take any chances.

The bell rang for lunch, and he packed away his books and turned to face Derek.

"Lunch in the cafeteria today," Chad stated.

"I never go there. I always go to the library."

"Today is different. High schools are vicious rumor mills, and the sooner we satisfy everyone's curiosity, the sooner they'll move on to the next people."

Derek scrubbed his hand across his face. "You're not suggesting ...like ...that we ...? I don't know, Chad."

"Look, Derek. I've never done this before either. I've never come out to anyone at school, but I don't want to hide away anymore. Not when it comes to being with you."

Chad lifted Derek's bag, threw it over his shoulder, and held out his hand for Derek to take. He wiggled his fingers until Derek nodded his head and took his hand.

The walk down the hallway to the cafeteria was like a scene out of a surreal, slow-motioned movie. As they moved down the hall, with their hands tightly clasped together, a hush fell over each section as they passed through it. There were whispers behind covered faces and a lot of nasty remarks, but to Derek's surprise, there were also a few people that patted them on their backs, offering encouraging words.

When they finally arrived at the cafeteria, Chad picked a table in the back corner of the room.

"See, that wasn't so bad, was it?" Chad laughed as he tried to control his breathing.

Derek gripped tight to the table, facing straight ahead. He had no further interest in witnessing the commotion they'd caused.

"Just give me a minute until my heart restarts," he said.

"God, I could kiss you right now."

"Please don't." Derek smiled and leaned over the table, supporting his head on his hand. "I've never met anyone quite as brave as you."

"That's not bravery, that's vanity. Golden boy, remember." Chad shrieked when Derek kicked him under the table but quickly composed himself as he realized people were staring.

"It's called false bravado," he added. "Fake it until you make it. I'm sure you've heard of it before."

"I didn't think people actually fell for that stuff."

"Who's falling for stuff? I'm living the dream. Dashing, young football star finds gay love with unlikely, but hot and gorgeous history partner."

"You're impossible."

"Does that mean you'll keep me?" Chad reached for Derek's hand. "Because I really want to be your boyfriend."

Derek sighed in exasperation. Chad was incorrigible. Incorrigible and incredible. He took Chad's hand, not caring who around them was watching.

The store was unusually busy for a Thursday night, but Derek was glad. It was keeping his mind off what would technically be his third date with Chad. He finished ringing through the last sale of a rush and headed over to the dressing rooms to make sure they'd been cleaned out. He reached up to retrieve some hangars off a rack and shrieked as one of his co-workers Cindi snuck up behind him and grabbed him.

"You've been awfully quiet tonight," Cindi said. "What's up?" She took the handful of hangars off Derek and stepped into the back room with them.

"I have a date tonight." Derek held the door open for Cindi until she came back out into the store.

"Who's the lucky guy?"

"Funny story. It's Evelyn Parker's son."

"No fucking way!" Cindi covered her mouth and lowered her voice, and moved Derek with her, away from the customers. "I thought Evelyn only had the one son. The quarterback."

"That's the one." Derek pulled Cindi down behind a rack of slacks when she shrieked loudly. "Cindi, jeez, you're going to get us both fired."

"Oh, Derek, when I was in high school, I always dreamed of dating a quarterback. I'm so jealous." Cindi popped back up and pretended to be refolding some sweaters that apparently needed two people to manage them. "So, is he really hot?"

"He's coming here to pick me up. You can judge for yourself. But he totally makes me weak in the knees."

"Baby, I'm so happy for you. You tell him to treat you right, or he'll have to answer to me."

"Yeah, I can see it now. Barbie doll chastises quarterback for breaking the heart of the lonely, but well dressed—"

"That is not going to happen." Chad stepped up behind Derek, grabbed him around the waist, and pulled him close, kissing the back of his neck.

Derek came very close to swooning.

"Cindi," he said. "This is Chad. Chad, Cindi."

"Cindi. Yeah, hey," replied Chad. "My mom has mentioned you. She says you make her laugh. I think that's a good thing." He shrugged and smiled at her.

Cindi just nodded her head.

"You're early," Derek said. "I still have another twenty-five minutes until I'm off." He reluctantly removed himself from Chad's arms. "Can you amuse yourself without getting into trouble?"

"I should be able to manage that." Chad snuck a quick kiss before wandering away. He motioned for Cindi to follow him and waited until Derek was out of earshot before he stopped and turned to speak to her. "Where do you keep the staff measurements?"

"They're behind the till," Cindi replied. "What are you up to?" She clapped her hands together excitedly. "Can I help?"

"I just want to grab Derek a few things. If he has anything on hold, we'll start there. He needs a few jackets. Different lengths and colors. Oh, and that new fall line from that Japanese guy you carry. We'll grab him a few outfits from that."

Chad circled around the store and attempted to point out clothing items, inconspicuously, for Cindi to tag. He ended up in the shoe department perusing through their men's shoes and boots.

"Cindi, I can't decide," Chad said. "Could you maybe send one of everything in brown and black to the house for me? He can go through them and use what he wants."

"Cindi, we have customers." An attractive woman with a very tight face approached and touched Cindi lightly on the arm before turning to address Chad. "Son, might I suggest you find a store more suited to your tastes. Perhaps sporting goods."

"Ms. Edelson ..." Cindi crossed her arms and tapped her foot impatiently.

"No, that's all right, Cindi," Chad said. "You've been very helpful. Could I get my delivery sheet off you before you go, or I'll forget what I'm buying" He took the wad of papers from Cindi and winked mischievously at her.

"Or sheets! My goodness, but I've gone a little crazy," Chad turned to face who he assumed was the store manager, "haven't I, Ms. Edelson? How much do you think this adds up to?"

Chad sat down, delicately crossing his legs for effect and pulled out his phone, and started adding up what he'd picked out so far.

"This is all very amusing," Ms. Edelson said, her impatience becoming obvious. "But you need to leave the store."

"That can't be right," Chad said, then clicked his tongue dramatically in feigned confusion. "My entire bill is only twenty-three thousand dollars, give or take. I'm positive I selected more than that." He scanned the sheet again and shook his head in disgust. "Some of these items must've been on sale. Which is absolutely unacceptable. I won't have my boyfriend wearing sale items."

He slammed the sheets down on the chair beside him. "Where's Cindi? We need to straighten this out immediately!"

"Chad, what are you doing?" Derek grabbed the stack of delivery sheets off the chair and looked them over with a smile on his face. Everything was in his size, not Chad's.

"I'm shopping," replied Chad. "You told me to stay out of trouble until you finished work."

"I didn't mean for you to buy out the whole fucking store."

"Derek, do you know this young man?" Ms. Edelson asked.

"Yeah, he's ...my boyfriend." Derek bumped Chad with his hip and laughed when Chad hugged his legs. The guy was truly incorrigible.

"When can I have all this stuff delivered?" Chad took the papers from Derek's hands and handed them to Ms. Edelson.

"You're not seriously planning on buying all this stuff for me?" Derek asked as he stepped away from Chad.

"Sure, why not?"

"Because that's a lot of money."

"It's a drop in the bucket. My mother has done far worse than that on a single outfit."

"I have nowhere to put all this. You saw the size of my house."

"I'll set you up with your own closet at my house."

Derek tightened up as a wave of anxiety overtook him.

"Chad, it's too much," he whispered.

"Please, let me buy it for you," Chad said. "I was horrible to you last night." He stood, brushed his hand across Derek's cheek, and pulled gently on one of the curls along the side of his face. Unsuccessful, he began drawing slow circles on Derek's arm and pouting at him, finally prompting a shy smile to cross Derek's face.

"Ms. Edelson," Derek said. "Could you put Chad Parker's purchases on his mother's account and have everything sent to the address on file. It's nine, so I'm off now. I'll see you on Saturday."

He smiled at her smugly and grabbed onto Chad's arm as Chad led him from the store and into the parking lot.

"You're insane, you know that, right?" Derek said once they'd cleared the store.

That's a distinct possibility," Chad replied. "So, where do you want to go now?"

"Wait. How was the game?"

"Not very exciting. The other team was no match for us, but I still managed to come away with a nasty bruise on my ribs, thanks to Zeek supposedly fumbling the ball."

He lifted his shirt, grinning as Derek cringed then brushed his fingers across the purple welt. "You'll have to kiss it better for me."

"Maybe later." Derek let his hand linger on Chad's ribs as he gazed up into his eyes, but then looked away. He still wasn't sure about Chad. He seemed too good to be true.

"Hey, is that Sam and Tyler over there? And Gus?" Derek said then spun in place, gripping tight to Chad, alarmed to see Dillon leaping through the bushes off to one side of them.

"Derek," Chad said, his voice harsh and laced with panic.

Derek blinked. What on earth was going on?

"When I tell you to run," Chad continued. "I want you to get to my car over there as fast as you can and lock the doors. Here are the keys." He pushed the keys into Derek's hand and wrapped his arms protectively around him.

"What's happening?" Derek asked.

"Shh …just trust me."

Derek was very aware that Chad was shaking badly as he held him. He felt Chad rummaging around behind him and almost dropped the cell phone Chad pushed into his hand. Then almost dropped it again when he saw Sam and Tyler come flying across the parking lot toward them.

"This is it." Chad quickly kissed the back of Derek's head. "Run! Now!" He pushed Derek away from him and toward his car. "Sam, cover Derek!" He looked over his shoulder. "I'll get Zeek." He took off at a run and climbed over a couple of cars before leaping off one of them to tackle Zeek, who was making his way toward where he and Derek had been standing.

Derek struggled with the electronic locks for a second and then slipped into the driver's seat as Sam raced up behind him. Sam motioned down through the front windshield for him to lock the doors, and patted the top of the car as he heard the locks engage.

He lost sight of Sam momentarily until he looked out the passenger window. Sam had been tackled by Marlboro, Pete and some other guy that Derek didn't recognize, and they were punching and kicking him. Vicious. Unrelenting.

As he watched in horror, Derek began shaking and crying. He peered out the driver's window, trying to spot any sign of Chad, but he couldn't see him anywhere.

Fumbling with Chad's phone, Derek wiped the tears away from his eyes before turning it on and dialing '9-1-1'. It took less than three minutes for an ambulance to show up followed by a squad of police cars racing into the parking lot and dispatching themselves throughout the lot.

He'd pressed himself up against the passenger window trying to see where Sam had gone when there was a sudden, frantic knock on the driver's window. His heart started again when he saw it was Chad, with Sam in tow. He unlocked the door and waited until Sam crawled into the backseat before passing the keys to Chad.

"Where are the other guys?" Derek asked.

"They're in Tyler's car," Chad replied. "We need to get out of here before the police catch up with us."

Chad checked his rearview before pulling slowly out of his stall and easing the car along the aisles and turning sedately onto the street. Once they were a few blocks away, he floored it and took off toward his house.

"I heard you yelling Zeek's name?" Derek said.

"Yeah," Chad replied. "Zeek and a few of his thugs came to pay us queers a visit." He released the breath he'd been holding. "Fortunately, for us, the guys were following them after the game."

"And once again, jackass," Sam said. "It would be really helpful if you would remember to turn your phone on. Dillon was running all over the mall trying to figure out which store Derek worked in."

"It's the clothiers at the entrance," Derek said.

"Figures!" Sam rubbed Derek's head affectionately. "Not that it was a clothing store. But that it was at the entrance."

"Thanks again," Chad said as he peered over his shoulder at Sam. "I must owe you guys something fierce." He smiled when he saw Sam resting his hand on Derek's shoulder. It was monumentally important to him that his best friend accept Derek.

"Just buy me a tropical island someday, and we'll call it even," Sam said, and then pushed on the back of Chad's head.

"That might be tricky. But I could buy you a really nice yacht, and you could cruise around some tropical islands."

"The tab is still open. I could be looking for something more substantial by the time we get you through high school."

"Hah!" Chad pulled the car to the end of Sam's driveway and climbed out to let him out of the backseat. "I'm not going to school tomorrow. Make my apologies."

"Make your own fucking apologies. I'm planning on nursing my wounds and sleeping until lunchtime tomorrow." Sam pounded Chad on the back and began his limp up the driveway to his house.

"Damn, Derek, I'm sorry," Chad said as he peered into the car. "I was so distracted by everything. I forgot to head off in your direction before driving home." He slid into his seat and started up the car, but let it idle.

"That's all right," Derek replied. "I'll stay at your place. I don't think it's a good idea for me to go to school without you there."

"All right then."

Chad beamed and took off up the road. Sam's house was only a few doors away, and Chad was soon taking the last bend in the driveway as he approached his house. It was so late that no one came to escort them into the house, and Chad had to use a key to get in through the front door.

"I'll call someone to make up a room for you," Chad said. "I don't know why my mother doesn't have a few beds made up on spec, but she insists that sheets shouldn't sit on a bed for more than a day or two." He picked up a phone in the foyer and began dialing some numbers.

"Won't they be asleep?" asked Derek.

"That's all right. It's their job." Chad set the phone back down when Derek frowned at him. "What would you like me to do?"

"I actually wanted to stay in your room."

"Well, that is good news." Chad pulled Derek to him and kissed him, and then grabbed his hand, pulling him down the stairs.

"Don't get too excited," Derek said. "I'm just a bit freaked out after tonight." He stopped Chad outside his bedroom door. "This is going to sound really girlie, but I just want you to hold me tonight. Nothing else. You need to promise me."

"You're killing me, you know that?" Chad turned on a few small lights and threw back the covers of the bed before wandering into the bathroom. "Seriously, killing me."

Derek followed him and sat on the edge of the tub, while Chad cleaned the blood from his face. After he was finished, Derek could see that Chad only had a few small cuts and one large bruise on his cheek. He averted his eyes and shook his head as Chad relieved himself in full view of where he was sitting.

No shame.

"Chad. About what I said ..."

"I can do holding. Master of restraint right here." Chad turned to face Derek and crossed his arms. "But why do you have to be so fucking gorgeous? I could totally get lost in those eyes of yours."

"The answer is still *no*." Derek pulled himself up and shoved Chad out of the bathroom so he could use it in private, but Chad kept talking to him under the bathroom door.

"You know that is one of the downsides of liking guys," Chad said. "You think like us, or we think like you. Whatever. Flattery gets you nowhere. We all know the game."

Chad waited for a response from Derek, but after getting nothing, he crossed the room to his bed. He considered stripping off all his clothes before climbing in, but he knew that would really piss Derek off, so he left his boxers on.

He'd just fixed up the pillows and tucked himself under the blankets when he heard the bathroom light click off. He opened his eyes, watching Derek walking tentatively toward the bed.

He grinned when he saw the tight, pink and yellow underwear and light purple undershirt.

"I can't let you into my bed looking like that," Chad said.

"And why is that?" Derek threw his clothes onto a chair and turned off the light beside it.

"You don't match at all. Pink, yellow ...and then purple. I'm sorry, but one piece of your outfit has to go."

"Fine. Top or bottom. Your choice." Derek stood with one hand on his hip and eyed Chad anxiously.

"Because I really like you ...the top." Chad watched Derek pull the shirt off over his head and toss it onto the chair with his clothes. He shifted in bed as his body responded to what he was seeing. "Damn those hips of yours. I just want to grab onto them and—" He fell back on the bed and covered his head with a pillow. "Quick. Turn off the light and jump in before I stop breathing."

Derek turned the light off and carefully climbed in under the blankets. He pulled them up over his shoulders and tucked himself into the pillow. He would've preferred to wear his undershirt; he always got cold at night. But some part of him wanted things to move forward with Chad. His bare skin tingled with anticipation.

"Whoa," Chad whispered as Derek jumped and began shivering as he moved across the bed toward him. "Just holding."

Derek nodded, but held his breath as Chad's arm wrapped over him and pulled him close to his body. Chad's obvious arousal pressed into his back. He quaked against Chad's chest.

"You're seriously shivering," Chad said. "Let me get your shirt back. I'm so sorry." He threw back the covers and made to get out of bed. "I'm such a fucking idiot sometimes."

Derek touched Chad's arm to stop him.

"No," he said. "I think I'm more scared than cold."

"Scared of what? Tonight with Zeek?" Chad pulled the covers back up around them and held Derek to him.

"No."

"What ...me?" Chad kissed Derek on the shoulder and tucked him tighter against his chest, attempting to warm him with his body. "I made you a promise. I may come off as a brazen ass sometimes, but I respect your decision."

"Thanks."

He paused and took a deep breath.

"I've never actually had a boyfriend before," Derek continued then rolled over to face Chad to tell him more about it. He was taken aback when he realized how close they were to each other. Chad's warm breath rolled seductively across his lips. "Oh crap—" He couldn't stop himself. He grasped Chad's face and pulled him onto his mouth. So warm. So responsive.

More.

Chad returned Derek's advances but made sure he didn't encourage him to take it any further. He gasped, and his gut tightened when Derek's hands began to rove over him.

He grabbed Derek's hand before it moved too far down his body.

"Why are you stopping me?" Derek asked, breathing heavily. He pulled away, completely confused, and a little embarrassed. "I thought that's what you wanted."

"Before you got into bed tonight, you were adamant that you didn't want to have sex with me," Chad replied. "But then we start kissing, and suddenly you change your mind? Full points to whoever can figure out what brain you should be listening to." He played his fingers through Derek's hair and stroked the top of his ears. "I don't want you jumping into anything you're not ready for." He squinted at Derek. "You've never done it before, have you?"

"I told you I'd never had a boyfriend."

Chad wrinkled his eyebrows in the darkness.

"You don't need a boyfriend to have sex," he said.

"That's not my thing." Derek rolled over and pressed his back into Chad's chest, basking in the warmth that rolled across his neck.

"That doesn't surprise me. You're really special, Derek."

"So, you don't mind holding me like this?"

"No, this is actually kind of nice. Don't get me wrong. I'd rather be fucking you senseless right now. But this is nice."

"Such a romantic." Derek reached back and patted Chad lightly on the head before snuggling himself further into his chest. "Goodnight, Chad."

"Yeah, yeah. I'll see you in the morning." Chad kissed

Derek on the head and nuzzled his face into the back of Derek's neck. It was actually nice to hold him like this.

Chapter Five | Friday

"Chad, are you down here?" Evelyn called as she made her way down the hall toward Chad's bedroom. "The school just phoned, and they said you'd called in sick, and they wanted to check with me." Evelyn stepped into Chad's suite and straightened away a few things before knocking on his bedroom door. She was about to open it when Chad shouted out to her.

"Mom," he said. "I'm not going to school today. We ran into a little trouble last night when I picked Derek up."

"What kind of trouble?"

"Remember that guy, Zeek, I told you about on my football team? He and his friends decided to teach us a lesson. They jumped us in the parking lot at the mall."

"Chad, that's horrible." Evelyn opened the door and pulled open the curtains. "Oh, my god!" Her hands went up to her face, and she covered her mouth. "What happened to your face?"

"Part of getting jumped involves fighting, Mom. Luckily, the guys were there to save my ass, yet again."

"Those boys are priceless." Evelyn turned to look at Derek and sighed. "Derek, are you all right, sweetie?"

"Um, …yes." Derek pulled the blankets up until they were right under his chin, imagining how his mother would've reacted if she'd walked in to see him in bed with a guy. "Chad locked me in the car, so I wouldn't get hurt."

"The whole thing is unacceptable," Evelyn said. "I'm going to phone the school right now." She stepped through the door but poked her head back in. "Derek, your mother should phone as well. I'll give her a call. What's her number?"

"No!" Derek struggled against the covers. "Please don't do that."

"Nonsense," she answered. "It's not right that those boys should be permitted to continue bullying you, simply because you choose to be in a relationship with each other."

Derek shook his head.

"No," he said. "My parents don't know."

"That you're seeing Chad?"

"Yes. No. I mean …they don't know I'm gay."

"Well, that throws a curve ball into things." Evelyn paused. "Did you want me to speak with them for you? I'll be very tactful."

"Mom!" Chad sat straight up in bed. "Stop. Derek will tell his parents when he's ready."

"I'm just trying to help," Evelyn replied. "By the way, a large shipment of shoes and clothing was just delivered. I'm assuming it's for Derek because everything is too small for you."

"Thanks, Mom. Could you have Pierre set up a closet for Derek in the front guest suite? He doesn't have enough room at his place."

"Certainly. Did you remember to put it on my account? It's such a pain when you use your credit card for big purchases like that. The accountant ends up phoning me, looking for receipts to match up with the statement. It's ridiculous."

"Scandalous!" Chad grinned at his mom and tucked himself back under the covers, pulling Derek into his arms.

"You're making fun of me again. Do you two want breakfast in bed? I can send someone down with some Eggs Benedict."

"That sounds great, but we'll come upstairs for breakfast later."

Derek waited until he heard Chad's suite door close.

"Your mom is amazing," he said.

"She's pretty cool most of the time. A bit pretentious sometimes. But she always means well."

Derek yawned and peered around.

"What time is it?" he asked.

"Um …nine thirty. So, when do you think you'll tell your parents about me? I'd like to meet them."

Derek felt his heart skip a beat.

"No, you don't," he said. "Once you meet them, you'll be running and screaming to get away from them."

"But they raised such an amazingly brilliant and gorgeous son."

"Chad …"

"Damn it. It's a very bad habit of mine. I'm flawed."

"You're a flawed goof." Derek ran his hand down the side of Chad's face stopping at his lips before kissing them. "Is it all right if I stay here this weekend?"

Chad's eyes lit up.

"Absolutely," he said. "What's up?"

"My parents are both working, and I don't feel safe alone in my house. I work on Saturday though. Do you mind giving me a ride?"

"Sure. Hey, that means you'll be here for the game on Sunday. The whole team is coming over. Minus the intolerant ones."

"Oh goody. I'll stay in your room and do my homework."

"You're not real big on football, are you?"

"I don't mind it, but the idea of an entire team of football players leaping around watching a game sounds like a recipe for me getting trampled into your mom's carpet."

Derek moved the covers and climbed on top of Chad, pressing their chests together and shifting his hips, rubbing his morning erection against Chad's.

"Derek? What are you doing?" asked Chad, his hands immediately finding their way onto Derek's ass and gripping it.

"I want to take this thing in stages."

"I thought the answer was *no*."

"Thinking with the brain up here." Derek tapped his head and grinned. "I've changed my mind. But I want to take it slow over the next couple of days."

"Oh, I see. So, you're going to torture me for days, is that it?"

"Chad, please, you have no idea how scary this is for me."

Chad sighed.

"All right," he said. "We'll do it your way, but don't get mad at me if I turn into a completely frustrated jerk." Chad wrapped his arms around Derek's shoulders and rolled him onto his back. "But, I prefer to be on top."

"Do you really?" Derek grinned. "I never would've guessed."

"Mm …" Chad drew Derek's hands up over his head and interlaced their fingers before aggressively taking his mouth. He let their tongues linger seductively, leaving his heart racing with need by the time he pulled away to study the look in Derek's eyes. They were filled with wonder and desire; he was absolutely perfect.

"Damn it, Derek," he said. "This is going to be brutal."

"Please keep going. I'll tell you when to stop." Derek pulled his hands from Chad's grasp and ran them up into Chad's hair, pulling him back onto this mouth. His breath became rapid and shallow as Chad moved away from his lips and began running his tongue down the side of his neck, stopping to bite and kiss at his shoulder.

"You taste amazing," Chad said.

"I do?"

Derek gasped, in surprise, when Chad's hand found its way down his body. He sighed with desire as Chad began rubbing and stroking him hard. "Ah. Oh my god, Chad."

"Fuck, Derek—" Chad lifted his head and looked at Derek. "You're seriously disproportionate. You're going to make me a very happy boy by the end of this weekend."

"What?" Derek stared at him in confusion, but Chad had ducked under the blankets without answering to draw his lips across Derek's chest until he found what he was looking for. He playfully flicked Derek's nipple with his tongue and then took it into his mouth, sucking and biting it gently until he felt Derek arch up beneath him.

Chad moved to the other side and laughed softly as Derek moaned, prompting him to change directions and slowly work his way down Derek's stomach, kissing and licking his skin. He'd just reached the top of Derek's underwear when Derek's hand pulled at him to come back up.

"What's the matter?" Chad asked.

"You need to stop," Derek said. "I need you to stop."

"Seriously? I was just getting to the good part. Let me do this one thing for you at least. Please." Chad pouted at Derek and kept his hand below the covers, stroking him, until Derek nodded.

Grinning, Chad ducked back beneath the covers and removed Derek's underwear, making a production of throwing them across the room. Derek clutched at the sheets and braced himself, closing his eyes. He inhaled sharply as the warm touch of Chad's tongue circled the ridge of his cockhead. The sensation was incredible.

"Ah—" Derek bit his lip. Chad's mouth had begun caressing his shaft, and now Chad had taken him into his mouth completely, sucking and guiding him into his throat. He pressed his hips up.

"Sorry," Derek said, realizing what he'd done when he heard Chad gag. "I'm so sorry."

"Fuck …" Chad coughed, laughing, patted Derek on the thigh then took Derek back into his mouth, humming with contentment.

Derek stared up at the ceiling, hoping the increasing tension and stars were normal as he rode through the experience Chad was taking him on. He felt a familiar surge building within him and clutched at Chad's hair in desperation, to keep him from pulling away. He arched up, moaning, grinding, clutching, as the tension released down Chad's warm throat.

He could hear Chad laughing softly under the covers, and was startled when he felt Chad's tongue running over his skin, licking away any sign of the morning's activities. He grabbed Chad when he resurfaced, pulling him to his mouth, the remnants of his desire fueling him to consume the slickness covering Chad's lips.

As Derek's heart rate slowed, he relaxed and gazed into Chad's eyes. "That was seriously intense."

"I aim to please." Chad rolled onto his back and pulled Derek into his arms. "So, it's safe to say you'd want to do that again."

"Definitely."

"Good to hear," Chad replied and then examined Derek's expression. "Hey, do you mind helping me out?

You don't need to go down there or anything. I just need your hand."

"For what?" Derek rolled his eyes and smiled. "Oh …"

Chad touched his lips to Derek's, trembling as Derek's hand ran down his torso and tucked into his underwear. He kept his eyes locked on Derek's, enjoying the intimacy of what Derek was doing for him. He latched heavily onto Derek's mouth, moaning into Derek's throat as he shuddered to completion, soaking them both.

Derek immediately pulled away, drawing his hand up from under the covers, desperately peering around to find something to wipe it on.

Chad had to laugh.

"You're a bit squeamish, aren't you?" he asked.

"I'm sorry," Derek replied. "But I think we both need a shower."

"All right. Let's make a run for it and hope my mom doesn't decide to check on us again." Chad threw the covers off and flicked his boxers across the room before reaching for Derek's hand. He sighed when Derek hesitated. "What? I'm going to see you naked eventually. I had you in my mouth. How can you be shy after sharing something that personal?"

Derek pursed his lips, unsure.

"What did you mean earlier?" he asked. "The proportion thing."

"Are you serious?" Chad replied. "You're fucking huge. I had a hell of a time keeping my gag reflex under control."

"Jeez, Chad." Derek climbed out of bed, and took Chad's hand, dipping down to pick up his underwear on the way to the bathroom. "Some of the stuff that comes out of your mouth …"

He closed his eyes. He'd walked right into that one.

"You liked that, did you?" Chad asked, nudging Derek.

"Yes, but can we not talk about it?" Derek smirked as he grabbed a couple of towels and hung them on the hooks beside the shower. He waited until Chad finished testing the water temperature and then stepped in after him. "This is all new to me."

"I know." Chad brushed an affectionate thumb across Derek's cheek. "We'll take it slow. I promise."

Derek took the soapy cloth Chad passed to him and had Chad turn to face the wall so he could wash his back. As the suds started a trip down Chad's back, it struck Derek that he'd just spent an amazing morning in bed with a guy he really liked, and now they were showering together.

He smiled, feeling empowered, and turned Chad to face him, so he could devour his mouth and set about replaying the whole thing.

"How much longer are they going to be in there? That fucking shower has been running for almost an hour." Gus stood at Chad's suite door and hammered loudly. "Chad! Finish up with him already. We need to do a run, and I don't have any money."

He smiled when he heard the shower turn off.

"Nice going, Augustus," Sam said. "Chad finally meets someone he really likes, and you cut him short, so you can buy drugs. Your priorities are completely fucked up." He pulled open the fridge and took out a beer before throwing himself back onto the sofa to turn on the television. He looked up as Chad came out of his suite.

They'd been right. Derek must've been with him.

"Hey! Casanova!" Sam teased. "You finally emerged. And you look all bright, shiny, and new."

"Shut the fuck up." Chad stole the beer off Sam and took a long swig before sitting down on the sofa and handing it back to him. "There's a roll of mad money in the canister under the sink, Gus. Go crazy." He glanced over as Gus made a rush through the bar and jogged his way back up the stairs.

He shook his head. "One track mind, that boy."

"Where's Derek?" Sam asked.

"He's doing all sorts of fussy stuff with his hair. He actually keeps hair product and eye makeup in that little bag of his."

"So, how was it? Without too much detail, please." Dillon was reclining in the sofa beside them. He lit a joint and flipped over to pop a window open.

"We didn't really do much," Chad replied. "He's a bit spooked about the whole sex thing."

"Bad experience?" Dillon asked.

"No experience."

"Nice," Sam said, nodding his head. "There's nothing like showing a virgin the ropes."

"And how the hell would you know that, Sam?" teased Chad.

"I can dream, can't I?" Sam was about to put the can to his mouth, but stopped and stared at it. "Please tell me you brushed your teeth after giving him head."

"Give me the fucking beer, asshole." Chad pulled the beer out of Sam's hand and went to stand in the doorway to wait for Derek. He could only imagine how nervous Derek was about coming out of his bedroom, in front of his friends, with them knowing what they'd been up to all morning. He grinned. Then again …all afternoon. The entire day had been intense.

He peered further into his suite and saw Derek standing just inside his bedroom door. He motioned for him to join them, and Derek reluctantly crossed the room and stepped out into the lounge.

"Good morning," Sam said, smiling at Derek.

Derek lowered his eyes.

"Hey, Chad?" Dillon said. "Can we order pizza? I'm starving."

"Sure, go for it." Chad smiled and kissed Derek's forehead to calm him. He looked nervous. He pulled him close, hugging him, and whispered in his ear. "They don't care. And they certainly won't judge you. Sex is a normal part of any relationship. You have nothing to be ashamed of."

Derek sighed, gripping tightly to Chad's arm. "I know."

"Is Derek all right?" Dillon popped off the sofa and approached the pair. "I hope those guys last night didn't freak you out too much." He handed Derek the joint he'd been smoking. "I know you don't do this stuff, but you look like you could use it."

He grinned when Derek took a short drag without coughing.

"Thanks, Dillon," Derek said, handing it back. Then tucked his head into Chad's chest, and started to cry.

"Hey ...hey, no crying," Chad said. "What's wrong?"

"My emotions are all fucked up," Derek replied.

"Sex will do that to you sometimes." Sam passed by them on the way to the bar to get another beer.

"And once again," Chad said. "How the fuck would you know that, Sam?"

"I'm still dreaming over here." Sam raised a can in mock salute.

"Jeez, Sam. Way to make Derek feel awkward." Dillon patted Derek on the shoulder. "It could be because Zeek was after him last night." He tipped his head. "Or yeah ...could be the freaky Chad sex thing. That would do it." He pounded Derek on the back, laughing, and launched himself back over to the sofa to crash.

"Right," Chad said. "Derek and I are going to head upstairs to the kitchen for something non-alcoholic to drink while we wait for the pizza. You guys try and behave yourselves down here."

Upstairs, the expansive space filled with massive stainless steel appliances and white marble countertops was positively blinding. Derek circled around it, running his fingers along the counters and taking in the incredible detail involved in its overall design.

"Where's your fridge?" he asked.

"The main one is in here." Chad touched a cupboard panel, and a door sprung open revealing the largest fridge Derek had ever seen, and it was well organized and completely spotless. "It actually has two sides." He touched another panel and a fridge the same size as the first opened up. "But you wanted something to drink, and you won't find anything in here." He led Derek around a corner and showed him two 'floor to ceiling' height, glass front, beverage coolers. One was filled with wine bottles and the other with everything else possible. "We also have another big fridge in the larder for extra storage."

"You only have three people in your family. Why do you need such a huge kitchen and so many fridges?"

"Don't forget, we also have six live-in staff." Chad winked. "They have to eat sometimes too."

Derek shifted, uncomfortable.

"It sounds like a vicious cycle to me," he said. "You wouldn't need staff if your house wasn't so fucking big. And you wouldn't need such a big house if you didn't have so much fucking staff!"

Chad stepped back.

"Are you mad at me?" he asked.

Derek sighed and shook his head.

"Then what?" Chad asked.

"I'm just feeling a little overwhelmed."

"I'm sorry. Do you want to hang out at your house instead?"

"No, but I'd like to pick up a few things for the weekend later on today if that's all right."

"Let's go now. The guys can eat pizza on their own. Chances are they're going to be a complete pain. We can pick up burgers or something on the way."

"Awesome." Derek breathed through a sigh. "Please."

Derek fumbled his keys multiple times, as he tried to open his front door. He hadn't thought through the scenario that had Chad coming into his house with him to grab a few things. He braced himself for the certainty that the house was going to be a complete pigsty. He only hoped there wasn't any rotting food anywhere on the kitchen counters. Or anywhere else for that matter.

"Please keep in mind this is nothing like your house," Derek said. "And I am completely averse to living like this." He pushed open the door and stepped inside with Chad right behind him. It smelled disgusting compared to the fresh air of Chad's house.

"My room is this way," he said as he picked his way up the stairs through the mountains of magazines, clothes, and his mom's attempt at collecting recyclable items.

He stopped and looked back. Chad was standing in the middle of the living room, taking it all in.

"Chad?"

"Wow. When people say that one half doesn't know how the other half lives, they weren't joking. This is disgusting. It's like an episode of *Hoarders* in here."

"Thanks a lot, asshole." Derek stormed up the stairs, headed for his room. He threw open his closet with more force than necessary, annoyed, and began sorting through what he was going to need for the weekend. He leaned against the frame.

Maybe this was a mistake. Chad was so far out of his league, he might as well be straight. But the way Chad made him feel….

Derek shrugged off the doubt and concentrated. Task at hand.

Most of the clothes he was going to use were already at Chad's. He'd gone to check out the closet in the guest suite before they'd left, and he'd been stunned at some of the items Chad had picked out for him. The boy actually knew his way around fashion. Just refused to wear it.

He grabbed a bag from under his bed and went to his drawer to pick out some underwear and socks.

"I like pink on you best," Chad said as he stepped up behind him and grabbed his hips. "It shows off your gorgeous skin tone."

"You know …" Derek turned himself to face Chad and leaned back against his dresser. "If I close my eyes, you almost seem gay sometimes."

"My mom says I couldn't think straight if I tried." Chad kissed Derek on the cheek, then turned and began wandering around the room, checking out the photos and books, and pieces of memorabilia neatly placed around the room. "There's nothing wrong with your room. It's all clean and neatly organized. Your own little piece of sanity. Am I right?"

"You got it in one."

"How old were you in this picture?" Chad flopped down on the bed, a photo album in hand.

"I think I was five." Derek lay down on his stomach beside Chad and took him through all the photos in the book, including the embarrassing days of braces, glasses, and severe acne.

"We should hang out here for a bit before we go back to my place," Chad said. "Those morons are going to be completely baked and stupid for hours. I'm not in the mood. Do you have a radio in here we can listen to?"

"Yeah." Derek reached over Chad and flicked his clock radio on, almost falling off the edge of the bed. "Whoa. This bed is nowhere near as big as yours is. It's strictly a one person job unless of course, you're planning on stacking."

Chad grinned.

"Interesting idea," he said. "What time do your parents come home?"

"Not for another couple of hours." Derek rearranged himself, sitting up and straddling Chad's hips, and started to undo Chad's shirt.

Chad settled in, hands behind his head.

"What are you planning on doing after high school?" he asked.

Derek struggled with a stubborn button. "I'd like to transfer to the main store in Vancouver and then maybe take some business courses. Work my way up to management."

"I can totally see you doing that. You've got a good fashion eye, and you're brilliant."

"Why thank you." Derek leaned over and kissed Chad. "What about you? What kind of plan has your family got strategically mapped out for you?"

"Ah, yes. The plan." Chad sat up slightly so Derek could pull his arms out of his sleeves. "University. Business degree of course. And then my dad will, ever so cautiously, introduce me to the exciting world of hoteliers."

"I don't think that would be so bad. With it being a family business and all. Would you live in one of the hotels?"

"Probably. That's what my dad does when he's down there. Maybe we could see each other every once in a while if we're both living in Vancouver." Chad pulled Derek's shirt loose from his pants and lifted it up over his head before tossing it onto the floor.

"I'd like that." Derek shuffled himself down the bed and worked his mouth across Chad's chest and down to his stomach.

"Do you think we really would? See each other?"

"I hope so." Derek sat up to undo Chad's belt and smiled deviously as he grabbed onto Chad's pants and hauled them and his boxers completely off his hips, down to his knees.

"Slow down. We've got plenty of time." Chad threw his head back, moaning as Derek took him into his mouth. "Damn, you're good. Are you sure you haven't done this before?" His heart hammered so loudly in his chest, he almost didn't hear the front door close. "Derek. Someone's here."

"What?" Derek looked up. "Fuck. He's home early!"

"Derek! Whose car is that out front?" Derek's dad's voice came booming up the stairs. Derek only had time to leap onto Chad's body to cover him up before his dad threw his door open. "What the *hell* is going on in here?"

"Dad, get out!"

"Not until you tell me what *the fuck* is going on in my own house!"

"Dad, please. I will. Just get out!" Derek dropped his head onto Chad's chest as his dad slammed the door shut. "Fuck my life."

"Way to come out of the closet, Derek," Chad said and grinned. "Extra points for dramatic effect."

"Fuck off." Derek kissed Chad and climbed off. "Any pointers or nuggets of wisdom that you wish to impart?" He pulled his shirt back on and stood at the door, ready to open it.

"My mind is a complete blank right now, thanks to you." Chad watched Derek reaching to open the door. "Hey, wait for me." He struggled to pull his pants up and do up his belt. "You didn't think I was going to let you go down there on your own, did you?" He quickly did up the buttons of his shirt and tucked it into his pants. "You're my boyfriend. We're in this together."

A booming, "Derek!" reverberated through the door.

Derek cringed; his dad was becoming impatient with the delay.

Chad opened the door and led the way down the stairs. Derek's dad was furiously pacing around the living room being careful not to knock over any of the stacks of boxes, bags, and magazines that were scattered around the room. He stopped and glared at the boys.

"Please tell me I didn't see what I thought I saw up there," he started. "Because if I did …"

"What didn't you see?" Derek asked.

"Don't be a fucking smartass, Derek."

Derek braced himself as his dad stepped forward and slapped him hard across the face, almost knocking him to the floor.

Derek held a hand to his lip; it was bleeding.

"Whoa! Hey!" Chad yelled, lunging forward, his fists clenched at his sides. "You hit him like that again, and I'll bust your fucking head." He pulled Derek to him, tucking Derek's face protectively into his chest, and whispered, "Let's get out of here."

"It's all right," Derek said. "I'm used to it."

"Derek, that's not something you're supposed to get used to." Chad peered down into Derek's face. His gorgeous eyes had taken on a hardened, dark hue. But there was also fear building.

Derek's dad started up again. "I always knew there was something wrong with you. The fancy clothes and makeup. I should've beaten all that girlie crap out of you years ago, you worthless little shit. Now, look at you. Sucking some guy's cock like a fucking prostitute." He made a grab for Derek, only managing to take hold of his collar, ripping the front of his shirt.

Derek pushed away from Chad.

"Chad, you should go," he said. "I'll stay home this weekend."

"Like hell, you will," Chad said as he bundled Derek up the stairs to his room, and slammed and locked the door. "I want you to grab everything you can. We'll come back for your pictures and stuff some other time. This is absolute bullshit.

"But, Chad …"

"No. You're moving in with me."

"I can't just move in with you. I can handle my dad." Derek jumped as the first strike against his door rattled the walls, followed by, "Get out here you little slut!"

"This is fucking ridiculous," Chad said as he threw Derek's bag up onto the bed and started tossing clothes into it.

"Don't worry about the clothes," Derek said. "I don't want my dad destroying my other stuff. I'll just take the pictures and everything." He scanned the room, scooping what he could.

Chad made a sudden leap for the door when Derek's dad ran into it with his shoulder, cracking the frame. He forced his back against the door, bracing his feet against the edge of the closet.

"Hurry the fuck up, Derek," he said.

"Yeah …I am." Derek shoved his pictures, awards and small pieces of memorabilia in the bag with a few items of his favorite clothing, and zipped it up. He stopped to gaze around the room that had been his sanctuary for his entire life. In some small way, he was going to miss it.

The hinges on his bedroom door threatened to give way under his dad's repeated attempts to break the door down. Chad's shoulder was pressed heavily against it, but he was beginning to have difficulties keeping it in place.

"Are you ready?" Chad asked. "I can't hold him much longer."

"Let's go. What's the plan?"

"When I let go of this door …run."

It felt good to be driving away from a house he'd hated for as long as he could remember. They'd managed to sidestep his dad as he'd fallen into the room when Chad released the door, and they'd escaped to Chad's car before his dad had managed to catch up with them. Derek rested his head on Chad's shoulder, gripping tightly onto his arm and contemplating what this meant for their relationship. It had rapidly moved past a simple boyfriend situation.

"Derek, we need to get you a cell phone."

"Um …sure. Why?"

"So, you can call me."

"Right. Yeah. I'll grab one on Tuesday before work."

"Good. And …how old are you?"

"I'm eighteen as of last week. Why?"

"Oh man, I missed your birthday!"

"You didn't even know me last week, dumbass." Derek shoved Chad playfully and then tucked back against him.

"Still. Do you have a driver's license?"

"Yeah, why?"

"Nothing. What's your favorite color?"

"I don't know. Red, maybe yellow."

"Wow. Those are a bit loud."

"All right, purple is up there as well, or classic black. What's with the twenty questions? Are you going to buy me more clothes, because I really don't need anything?"

"No, not clothes." Chad clipped his phone into the dash and called up a number. It rang twice before someone picked up.

"Hi, Monte speaking."

"Hey, Monte, it's Chad Parker."

"Chad, buddy. I was starting to think you'd forgotten about me. Have you made any decisions yet?"

"Yeah, I've been busy. Listen, I have my boyfriend here on speaker with me."

"Your boyfriend? Jeez, Chad. Wonders never cease with you. I wouldn't have known. I mean, congrats."

"Um, …thanks. Hey, it was his birthday last week."

"Say no more. What color do you want?"

"Black is my first choice, but we can work down through red, purple, and …yellow." He turned and looked at Derek, raising his eyebrows in feigned alarm at his color choices.

"All right, it doesn't come in purple or yellow. I'd have to order in a black, but I have a red one that I could have ready for you in a few hours."

"I'll be there in twenty minutes."

"Yes, sir. I'll have it ready in twenty minutes."

"As usual, it's a pleasure doing business with you, Monte. I'll put in a good word with my dad."

"Much appreciated. See you soon."

Derek leaned forward, confused, no stunned, as Chad ended the call and brought up the GPS screen on his dash.

"Chad, please tell me you didn't just buy what I think you did."

"I can't be driving your sorry, but cute ass everywhere. And I'm pretty sure the bus isn't your favorite mode of transportation. You need to be able to get to work, and my house is a hell of a lot further away from the mall than yours was. It's a very practical birthday present."

"So, what kind of *practical* car are we talking about?"

"It's one of those new Porsche convertible roadsters."

"Shut the fuck up."

"Fine. I won't speak." Chad smiled over at Derek and reached for his hand. "They're actually very practical cars. They rarely break down. They don't need to be serviced very often. And they last forever. See. Practical."

Derek shook his head and fell back into his seat. "Says the man with the unlimited budget to buy one in the first place."

"No. Not true. I have a number I can't go over every month. I've totally blown it this month, but I usually don't spend even a fraction of what's been allocated, so cumulatively speaking, I'm still good."

"Why are you doing all this for me?"

"I just want you to be happy. And have what you deserve." Chad turned and smiled over at Derek. "You really are beautiful."

Derek narrowed his eyes. "Mm …hm."

"So can I borrow your car sometime?"

"Hah! The way you drive. I know you bought it, but there's no fucking way you're touching my car."

Chapter Six | Saturday

It was late morning, and Chad and Derek were taking breakfast in the sunroom. Derek smiled, remembering Chad's mom coming into their bedroom that morning asking them where they were going to be *taking* their breakfast. He'd immediately had images of them wandering around the massive house with their breakfast on a tray trying to figure where to *take* it.

Derek smiled shyly over at Chad and was rewarded with a wink. He fiddled with his plate and then reached across the table for a banana. He smiled deviously at Chad as he peeled it and proceeded to eat it very slowly, making sure to take in all the flavors with the tip of his tongue. He could see Chad's knee bouncing up and down under the glass table as he finished it, seductively licking his lips. He knew he was torturing Chad a little, but he'd decided he wasn't going to hold out any longer. His heart was sending him all sorts of intense and exciting messages, and he wanted to talk to Chad about them tonight. He knew one thing for sure though. He'd be giving himself to Chad completely tonight.

"I have to get ready for work," Derek said.

"You don't have to leave for another hour."

"It takes me a while to get done up." Derek stood and dropped his napkin onto his plate. "I'll be sure to find you before I leave."

"Oh, no you don't," Chad said, standing. "You're not running off on me that easy. Not after that little banana number."

"Whatever do you mean?" Derek fluttered his eyelashes teasingly. "I was simply enjoying my breakfast."

He laughed and shrieked as Chad hoisted him over his shoulder and carried him back downstairs. Predictably, the space was littered with the bodies of Chad's friends.

"Dammit." Chad stepped over Dillon, who had passed out on the floor of the lounge, and headed into his suite; Sam was out cold on his bed.

"Fuck. Do you want to go swimming?" Chad asked as he dropped Derek into his arms. "No one ever goes in there, and there are lounges to lay on and everything."

"I really do have to get dressed for work." Derek readjusted his robe as Chad set him down, and reached up to kiss him. Then he released him. "Hold that thought until tonight ...I'm ready."

"Like ready, ready?"

"Yeah. You have to promise to be gentle with me though."

"Absolutely." Chad cupped Derek's face and lingered a smooth kiss on his lips. "You'll be home by like what? Ten, right?"

"Maybe by nine thirty." Derek gripped Chad's hand and looked up into his eyes. "One request though. Can you make sure your friends aren't here?"

"Done. I will be kicking them out and locking the doors at the first opportunity."

"All right. I'll see you when I get home." Derek kissed Chad, basking in the promise of what their night together would mean to both of them, then ran off to get ready for work.

Derek's shift seemed to crawl by. There were very few customers for a Saturday, and the only thing breaking up his day and making it interesting was taking Cindi out for a ride in his new car at every available break. They'd left for their half-hour meal break together and made a beeline for the car so they'd have time to grab something to eat and head to the beach.

Cindi insisted on having the top down even though it was absolutely freezing out, forcing Derek to crank up the heat to compensate. They were having a good time though, eating their lunch, and chatting.

"So," Cindi said as she chewed noisily. "He buys you a closet full of expensive clothes, a kick-ass sports car, and now you've moved in with him. And you've known him how long?"

"Including today." Derek lowered his voice. "Six days."

"And you don't find that odd?"

"Chad is a *live large* kind of guy. He's unstoppable really."

"But, Derek, sweetie ...you're not worried."

"About what? That he's some kind of bizarre, possessive freak? Yeah, it ran through my head, but I don't see it."

"What if he's some kind of sadistic, deviant pervert and he's trying to lure you in with gifts?"

"Then call me Hansel. But I'm pretty sure I can trust him."

"Oh, Derek, I hope you're right. I worry about you sometimes. You're such a lovely person, and you've been treated so horribly."

"You're sweet, Cindi, thanks, but I think I may have gotten lucky with Chad." Derek shifted in his seat and took a deep breath before continuing. "Can I share something with you?"

"Sure thing. I'm always here for you."

"See the thing is. I'm a virgin. And I'm planning on giving myself to him tonight."

Cindi popped her thumb out of her mouth, after cleaning off a glob of mayonnaise. She shook her head. "Hun, I'm not really familiar with the mechanics of that."

"I'm not looking for instructions." Derek laughed and started packing up the garbage from their lunch. "I was just wondering if you remember your first time."

"Yeah. It was horrible. And awkward."

"Great, something to look forward to." Derek started up the car and began backing out of the stall.

"Hold on, let me finish," Cindi said, tucking her hands into her lap. "That was the first time, but as the night progressed it got better and better, and by the next day, it was exquisite."

"Hm, I hope you're right. The problem is I have no idea what I'm supposed to be doing. And Chad ...well, he's been around the block more than a few times."

"But he's only eighteen. He's still a baby."

"Yes, but remember, he's also the *live large* guy." Derek pulled onto the street and headed back toward the mall. "I'm a little nervous and freaked out."

"Sweetie, if he really likes you as much as you say he does, you could do it completely ass-backward—" Cindi shrieked and snorted at her own joke as she pounded on the dashboard. "I'm sorry, I couldn't resist."

"That's why I love you." Derek smiled and shook his head, and turned into the parking lot of the mall.

"Anyway. If Chad really likes you, he won't care what you're doing as long as you're there, in the moment, doing it with him."

"Thanks, Cindi. That was actually pretty insightful. Are you sure you're really a blond?" Derek shrieked as Cindi punched him. They were going to be late. Again. He finished locking up the car so he could run into the store ahead of her. He beat her there by mere seconds, laughing and wheezing as they fell through the door.

The bedroom was almost the way Chad wanted it, but he needed to make a few more additions so it would be perfect. He'd sent someone out to the local florist to buy up every red rose they had; he just hoped Derek wasn't allergic to flowers.

He sighed with the realization that he really didn't know Derek very well. There were so many things that he still wanted to find out about him. The last of the boxes of candles were being dropped off in the lounge, so he went out to gather them up. He needed to finish placing them around the room.

"Chad, sweetheart," Evelyn said as she came down the stairs. "What is all this about? I was told that you sent out for boxes of red roses as well?" She grabbed a box of candles and followed Chad into his bedroom. She stopped, admiring the detail with which her son had decorated his room. "It's beautiful. You've done a lovely job. What's the occasion?"

"Candid moment, Mom?"

"Of course." Evelyn looked around and found a chair that hadn't been used in the overall display. "Hit me."

"Derek is a virgin, and he's entrusting me with that tonight. I want to make his first time special, but I'm not entirely sure how to do that."

"Oh—" Evelyn rose back onto her feet. "Well, you've made a good start of it by showing him how important this is to you. You've put a lot of thought into what you've done here." She opened up the box she'd been carrying and began placing more candles around the room, making sure only to set them where she was directed to by Chad. "Derek is quite different from the other boys you've dated in the past. They were all very rough and tumble like you, and I can only imagine how that would've played out in the bedroom. Although I'd prefer not to ..."

"Mom, believe me, most of the time, there was no bedroom ...or any kind of room involved."

"Too candid."

"Sorry."

"Chad. Derek is delicate and gentle, and innocent. You need to remember that. And you need to be patient with him." Evelyn set the last candle down and stood in front of her son, holding his face affectionately in her hands. "I'm going to take some liberties based on what I've observed and say that this is more than just sex to him. This is important to him. You're important to him. He may not realize it, but his heart is involved, and you need to be careful with it."

She kissed Chad on the forehead and patted him on the cheek before dropping her hands. "I noticed there are a lot of his things in your sitting area? Is there a reason for that?"

"Yeah, I meant to tell you about that. Derek moved in yesterday." Chad moved toward Evelyn when she crossed her arms. "Mom, you should've seen his house. It was horrible, and his dad. His dad beats him. He couldn't stay there."

Evelyn exhaled through her nose.

"So you decided to pull him away from his family?"

Chad squinted at his mom. This wasn't like her. To question him about his relationships. She trusted him.

Didn't she? But ...what if?

No. He was holding his ground.

"He doesn't need them," he said. "He's got me."

"Chad, are you listening to yourself? Are you planning to support him all the way through to graduation? Because that's what you've signed up for by moving him in here."

Chad lowered his gaze. She was right.

"I hadn't really thought it through that way," he said.

"You didn't think it through at all. When you bought Derek all those clothes, I didn't think much of it. You've always been very generous. But when you bought him that expensive car yesterday, I started to become concerned. And now …now you tell me he's moved in with you. You've only known the boy since Monday."

Chad dropped into the closest armchair. "I don't know what happened. It all made sense at the time."

Evelyn crossed the room toward her son.

"Chad," she said. "I need you to sit and think it through again. If this is what you want, your father and I will be behind you. And if you decide you've made a mistake, we'll fix it."

Chad scrubbed both hands through his hair and settled his elbows on his knees, staring down at the carpet.

This had all gone so horribly wrong.

"Jeez, Mom," he whispered. "What the hell have I done?"

Chapter Seven | Sunday

The police cars started arriving shortly after midnight. Protocol dictated that the interested parties had to wait for twenty-four hours before filing a missing persons report, but the department had waived the waiting period as a special favor to Carl Parker. He'd contacted them just after eleven-thirty to report that his son's boyfriend hadn't come home after work and they suspected he'd become the victim of a hate crime.

After a few calls were made, Derek's car was located a few blocks away from the store where he worked. It had been demolished and torched, but there was no trace of Derek.

The police collected up a few photos they found in Chad's possession. They eventually left just after four in the morning with little advice, except to phone the police if anyone heard from him.

Chapter Eight | October

The view didn't change much from day to day other than the gradual loss of foliage that was happening throughout the forested area of the estate. Chad was sitting where he always sat, and where he now slept, in the corner of the L-shaped sofa by the window in the lounge. He refused to go into his bedroom, and he wouldn't let anyone in to clean up the now rotting rose petals that he'd carefully sprinkled all over his bed for his night with Derek.

Derek had been missing for a month now, and there were no leads on who might've taken him or what might've happened to him. Chad had spent countless days crying and punishing his fists on the walls of the lounge for letting Derek drive himself to work that day, lamenting over how Derek would be home with him right then if he'd watched over him more carefully.

The pain of guilt was particularly excruciating as he thought about how if he'd just kept his hands to himself like his friends had told him to, Derek might be safe.

But then he would've missed out on getting to know the most amazing person he'd ever met.

Chad refolded his blanket and adjusted himself so he'd have a better view out the window. For the first couple of days, after Derek went missing, he'd held out such hope for his return that he'd imagined seeing him cross the lawn toward the window on several occasions.

The hallucinations had been so vivid, he'd leaped up to go outside and greet him, to hold him. But Derek was never there.

He turned over, pulled Derek's sweater to his face, and continued looking through the pictures in Derek's photo album, attempting to piece together what he'd lost.

Chapter Nine | November

There had been a light frost that morning, making the now barren trees glisten in the sunlight. Chad pulled the blankets up around his shoulders and tucked himself back into the corner of the sofa. His eyes were bloodshot after a particularly difficult night of retracing everything that he and Derek had ever said to each other, ending with Derek's final words of, "I'll see you when I get home."

He rolled over and stretched himself out. He'd promised his mom that he'd get a shower today. He'd let the cleaning staff into his room yesterday to clean up the rose petals and remove the candles, but he didn't want to go in there yet. It brought back too many memories of the conversations he and Derek had shared while lying in bed; he'd have to go upstairs to have a shower again.

His mom had asked him to join her upstairs for breakfast the day before and had set him to the task of trying to understand the reasons behind why he was feeling so much loss for a person he barely knew. She'd given him a journal to write in and had asked him to write down everything he did know about Derek and how those things translated into his feelings for him. It had been a difficult thing to do and had probably contributed to his horrible sleep the night before, but he glanced down at the journal and flipped through the entire one hundred pages; they were all full.

His mom had come down earlier that morning, briefly reading a few pages, and had been reduced to tears.

Chapter Ten | December

The snow was falling softly but building up fast, making the estate look pristine and new. Chad pulled an extra sweater on over his head and sat down on the sofa beside Sam.

"It's fucking cold in here," Sam said. "Is your furnace bust again or something?" He hauled the blanket out from underneath Chad and wrapped himself up in it.

"Yeah, the stupid thing has gone haywire. My dad's firing up the wood burning furnace, but I don't think we'll get much heat down here. It'll find its way upstairs. Heat rising and all." Chad pulled up the edge of the blanket and stuffed his feet underneath Sam's.

"Hey, get your freezing cold feet away from me." Sam shoved Chad over and wrestled him for control of the blanket, hoping to force a reaction from Chad. Something he never grew tired of after all the years they'd known each other.

Of course, Chad responded. "It's my blanket. Get your own."

"No way. Share."

Sam launched himself for an attack. Tickling worked best, but a bout of wrestling usually resolved any issues between them.

"Whoa." Chad coughed and gasped as Sam landed on him, knocking the wind out of him.

"Sorry …" Sam stopped, his face mere inches from Chad's, and just stared at him for a second. Then laughed and started tickling.

Chad grunted and tensed, and gripped Sam's wrists. He wasn't in the mood. "Enough. Get the fuck off me."

Sam slid off him. "Yeah, sure."

"What do you want to drink?" Chad asked as he leaped up and headed for the bar. "Beer, vodka. Hot chocolate?"

"Make me one of those polar bear things." Sam slumped against the cushions and flicked through the channels, eventually deciding on an old horror movie. "So, do you think you'll go back to school for second semester?"

"Yeah, my mom has me doing online schooling right now, but I think it's actually harder than taking the same course at school."

Chad carefully measured the Schnapps and Irish Cream into the mugs and added the hot chocolate he'd mixed up. He fished around in the fridge and pulled out a refillable canister of whip cream that, more often than not, was used as a weapon in a food fight, rather than its intended purpose. He grabbed the chocolate sprinkles off the back shelf and added those before throwing in a couple of tiny straws. "Thanks for coming over today. I know I can be a bit of a downer sometimes." He set the drinks down on the coffee table and curled himself back up on the sofa, and gently pulled part of the blanket away from Sam to cover his legs.

"As long as you don't start crying again. We're all good."

"No crying, I promise." Chad took a deep breath and tried, unsuccessfully, to set his mind on what was happening in the movie. "Do you think it's possible to be connected to someone by some kind of cosmic chain?"

Sam set his mug down. "A what?"

"You know. Some kind of connection that binds you to someone permanently. So you can always feel them with you."

"Fuck, Chad. You have to let him go. I hate seeing you tearing yourself up like this every day."

"It was just a thought." Chad took a large sip of his drink now that it had cooled down. "Oh, hey. Guess what I'm getting for Christmas this year?"

"I'm sure I can't imagine. What?"

"A chalet at Whistler. How cool is that? I think we should head up there for the entire winter break and hit the park every day." Chad shoved Sam. "And get this ...it has a hot tub built for twenty. Do I hear a party coming on or what?"

"Now, that is the Chad I know and love. That is definitely the winter plan. Who knows? I might even get lucky."

"My mom says you should never pin your hopes on a star, Sam ...fucking unattainable." Chad shrieked as Sam launched into a new tickle assault.

Chapter Eleven | January

The winters weren't nearly as cold in the valley as what they used to be back in the pioneer days. Chad had heard stories from one hundred years ago telling of minus fifty weather and the use of horses and sleighs to cross the frozen lake. It definitely wasn't like that now. He'd asked Sam to drive him to the beach where he was now looking out across the completely unfrozen lake.

"What exactly are we looking at?" Sam sat on the hood of his car, thankful for the warmth it was providing to his backside. It wasn't that cold out, but every once in a while the wind would pick up, and he'd be reminded that it really was wintertime.

"The passage of time," replied Chad.

"What kind of philosophical shit have you been reading now?"

"No, it's my own observation. It's likely that someone stood in this very spot and stared out at the lake one hundred, two hundred, even a thousand years ago. It's barely changed. But people have come and gone like flashes of tiny sparks over a fire. And it probably doesn't even realize we've been here."

"Holy fuck, you're cracking up. I swear." Sam went to stand beside Chad and nudged him with his shoulder. "It is pretty freaky how fast things can change though."

"Yeah, this whole thing with Derek has really made me appreciate the people in my life more." Chad affectionately threw his arm around Sam's shoulder and hauled him to his side. "You're my best friend, you know that? I can't imagine being without you." He let go of Sam and gave him a friendly ruffle of the hair before heading back to the car.

"Well, I'm sure I'd do just fine without you," Sam retorted.

"That's cold, Sam." Chad dropped into the passenger seat and turned up the heat when Sam started the car. "Do you think we'll still be friends when we're like, ninety?"

"Do you really think we'll live that long?" Sam looked over at Chad and smiled. "I could probably put up with you for that long."

"Good, because I have a feeling you're going to be stuck with me for a while." Chad turned in his seat to face Sam. "My dad asked me to speak with you about setting up an interview."

"What for?" Sam pulled into the drive-thru lane of their local hamburger place and placed their usual order.

"He's considering training you to be my associate or something. I'm not quite sure what it would be called, but you'd attend university with me and take all the same classes, and when we're finished, you'd come to work with me."

"It sounds like I'd be your babysitter." Sam fished around in his pockets and handed over some cash at the drive-thru window. He grabbed the bag and tossed it to Chad.

"No, not really," Chad replied, peering into the bag. "You'd end up with a master's degree in business, and you'd have your own job duties within the firm that would be completely separate from mine. But you're right, your primary function would be to watch my back, but you've already been doing that for years."

"Like I said. A babysitter." Sam pulled into a vacant spot at the back of the restaurant and shut the car off, but left the heat on.

"How many babysitters get paid seven figures?" Chad took a bite of his burger and watched Sam's eyes pop open.

"Are you fucking serious?"

"What can I say? Babysitting bad boys like me pays well." Chad threw a napkin at Sam. "Close your mouth. You're drooling."

"Why me?" Sam set his burger down on the dash and grabbed the napkin off his lap to clean the ketchup off his face.

"You've got impeccable grades at school, which will hopefully translate into good grades at university." Chad finished his burger, dug around in the bag and pulled out some fries. "It won't be a free ride. You'll be expected to work at a high level of proficiency within the firm. You really will become a fully functioning member of the management team. My dad wouldn't be considering you if he didn't think you could stand up to the rigors of corporate life."

"Jeez, Chad. I was planning on going to the local college and getting some crap office job. I'm not sure if I want to hang out with you and get paid millions of dollars to do it." Sam threw his head back on his seat and covered his face with his hands.

He dropped them suddenly and started laughing.

"See, I knew you'd come around." Chad flicked a fry straight into the side of Sam's head. "My dad is also impressed with your loyalty to me ...and so am I. You've always been there for me, Sam. No matter what kind of crap I get myself into, you're always there to dig me out of it."

"Someone has to do it. Jackasses like you are notoriously unable to take care of themselves."

"Well, it's a good thing I have you then." Chad beamed at Sam and clapped him on the shoulder, but he couldn't help but notice that Sam looked slightly troubled. He decided not to bring it up. If there were a problem, Sam would tell him about it.

Chapter Twelve | February

Chad pulled his car into the parking lot and stared over at the school. Today was the beginning of the second semester at Tekla, and he'd decided it was time to get back on track and finish high school. He gripped the steering wheel and leaned his head against the seat, sighing loudly.

"Are you ready for this?" Sam lifted his backpack from the floor onto his lap and prepared to open his door.

"I'm thinking about it."

"The bell is going to go any minute. Have you got your timetable already?" Dillon leaned in between the two front seats and looked out toward the school.

"Yeah, my mom picked it up yesterday," Chad answered.

"What's your first class?"

"English with Mr. White. The last class I had with Derek."

"Chad, you've got to stop doing this to yourself," Sam said. "You just keep digging at that pain. It's not healthy."

"I know, but I can't help it." Chad threw his door open and grabbed his backpack, but as he closed it a wave of emotion came over him. He hadn't driven his car since the day he'd moved Derek into his house. It had been a mistake driving it to school today. He jogged after Sam and Dillon and snuck in through the doors behind them. "Sam, can you come with me after school to get a different car? I think I need a change."

"Is this a Derek thing again?" Sam asked.

"Yeah. Please, man. Help me out."

"Anything for you, jackass." Sam smacked Chad in the head as he and Dillon ran past him on the way to their first class.

Chad took the stairs to the second floor and entered the English classroom through the back doors. The only available seat was at the table he'd shared with Derek in September. He looked around the room until he found someone he could easily push around and headed for him.

"I want your seat. Move." Chad grabbed this target by the shoulder of his shirt and hauled him roughly out of his chair.

"Fuck off. There's a seat at the back."

"I'm not sitting back there. Move asshole, before I make you."

"Mr. Parker. Is there a problem?" Mr. White stepped into the room, taking a seat behind his desk.

"I don't want to sit back there." Chad motioned to the back of the room and brusquely wiped a tear off his cheek with his thumb before resetting his composure and stance.

"Leonard, could you move to the back of the classroom, please," said Mr. White, waving his hand to dismiss any objections.

"Seriously!" Leonard grabbed his books and pushed past Chad. "Fucking football players. Get whatever they want."

Chad sighed and turned to the back of the room. "Hey, I'm sorry, Leonard. Thanks." Then sank into his seat and pulled out his books.

"It's nice to see you back, Chad," Mr. White said. "If there's anything else you need, you let me know, all right?"

"Thanks, Mr. White."

"All right, class. Today we are going to be reading a poem called *A Rose for Emily* by ..."

Chad zoned out as Mr. White spoke about the poem. He pulled out the worksheet he'd completed in September for that class and laid it on his desk, and pushed his binder out of the way so he could fold his arms on the desk, and lay his head down. It had suddenly occurred to him that they'd be watching a movie next class. The movie where he and Derek had held hands under the desk, and he'd realized his feelings for Derek were snowballing.

The bell rang for break and Chad stayed where he was, keeping his head on his arms, face hidden.

"How are you doing, son?" Mr. White asked.

"Terrible." Chad looked up to see that Mr. White had turned a chair around from the desk in front of him, and was leaning back in it with his arms crossed.

"There hasn't been any news at all?"

"It's like he dropped off the face of the earth. Even with all my dad's connections ...nothing."

"I know Derek came to mean a lot to you in that short space of time. I saw the way you looked at him."

"It was the weirdest thing. I've never felt like that about anyone before. Every time Derek looked at me ...my heart would stop."

"I'm so sorry, Chad." Mr. White sighed as the bell rang and gave Chad a friendly pat on the shoulder before heading back to the front of the classroom.

The rest of the day went agonizingly slow, and when the final bell rang, Chad snatched up his backpack and spilled out into the parking lot. He stumbled to his car and leaned against the door, waiting for Sam.

"Fuck. You look like hell," Sam said to Chad as he approached the car. "Do you want me to drive?"

"Could you? I want to head over to the dealership and pick out something completely different. You can have this car if you want."

"Most people trade in their old cars when they buy a new one." Sam caught the keys Chad threw to him. "I'd take you up on your offer, but we need to get this car out of your life."

"Yeah, you're right." Chad pulled the door open and stared down at the passenger seat. "Fuck, I can't sit there ..." He gripped the edge of the car, willing his knees to not give out. "Sam, I can't do this. Can you go pick something out for me? Just put it on my dad's account. I'll call Monte and let him know you're coming."

"Sure thing." Sam leaned against the car, resting his arms on the roof. "How are you going to get home?"

"I'll catch a ride with Tyler." Chad ducked down as Sam got into the car, looking in through the open passenger door. "I really appreciate this. You really are my best friend, Sam. I mean it." He patted the roof of the car. "I'll see you back at the house. I'll throw a few beers into the fridge with your name on them."

"Take it easy until I get there, all right?" When Chad nodded, Sam turned the car over and waited until Chad closed the door, then eased the car out of the parking lot.

Chad threw his shoes off and headed toward the bar. He rummaged around at the back of one of the cupboards and pulled out the bottle he was looking for and poured himself a drink. He checked to make sure the beer fridge was well stocked before grabbing the bottle he'd opened. He landed on the sofa and flicked the television on. After more than a few shots, he curled himself up and nodded off. By the time he woke up, it was dark outside, and Sam was sitting at the far end of the sofa, drinking a beer and watching television.

"Hey, sleeping beauty," Sam said. "I told you to take it easy. You've worked your way through half a two-six."

"Yeah, whatever. Is Dillon not coming over?"

"No, he decided it would be a good idea to do some homework for a change. He's actually starting to take graduation seriously."

"It's about time." Chad pulled himself off the sofa and headed to the bar to put the bottle away and grab a beer instead. "Did you get me some decent wheels?"

Sam grinned playfully. "Blew your budget entirely."

"Thanks. So when's your big interview with my dad?"

"Tomorrow. And I'm totally freaking out. I've known the guy since I was a little kid and he still scares the crap out of me."

"My dad has a tendency to do that to people, but don't sweat it. He likes you. I'm pretty sure it's a formality."

"So, he's really going to pay for my university as well?"

"Yup. And you'll get a big juicy contract with the firm when you finish. I bet Dillon wishes he'd smartened up sooner." Chad sunk down beside Sam and held out his can. "Here's to my future wingman and protector."

"Cheers to that." Sam tapped his can to Chad's and went back to scanning through the channels. "There's nothing on tonight. Do you want to order a movie?"

"I'm not really in the mood." Chad fell over onto Sam's shoulder and buried his face in Sam's sweater, and started to cry.

"Seriously?" Sam whispered.

"Being back at Tekla opened it all up for me again."

"Jeez, Chad. Enough crying already." Sam pulled his arm away and wrapped it around Chad, letting Chad rest against his chest. He stretched over, set his beer down on the table beside him, and tentatively lay his hand on Chad's head trying to soothe him.

Stroking Chad's hair lightly, Sam was relieved when he heard Chad sigh as he relaxed and stopped crying.

"It's going to be all right," Sam said as he stared down at Chad. "I promise." He took a deep breath, his heart hammering as he lifted Chad's face, and softly kissed him on the lips.

Chad immediately popped up out of his arms.

"What the fuck, Sam?"

"Nothing. I was just trying to be supportive." Sam shoved Chad away from him and headed to the bar to dump out the rest of his beer. "I need to get going. I have a lot of homework to do, and I need to prepare for your dad's interview tomorrow."

"Oh, no you don't. What the hell was that about?" Chad jumped up and joined Sam at the bar. "You kissed me."

"I told you. It was nothing. I've just had too much to drink is all." Sam turned to go, but Chad grabbed him by his arm.

"Like hell—" Chad pulled Sam back toward him and grabbed his chin, lifting his face to look at him. "And here I thought you were saving yourself for marriage or something."

"What? Fuck off. I'm not gay." Sam pushed Chad's hand away from his face and turned his back to him.

"Sam, you're a horrible liar. Your eyes get all twitchy."

"Just drop it, Chad. Please."

"Who are you hiding from? Me? Our friends? Jeez, you should know better than anyone that none of us would care if you're gay."

Sam turned, shrugging, stuffing his hands in his pockets.

"Just because it's easy for you," he said, "to be out there doing your thing, it doesn't mean that it's going to be easy for the rest of us. The whole thing has been eating me up for years."

"Why didn't you come and talk to me about it?"

"I didn't want you thinking I was coming on to you."

"And kissing me doesn't send that signal."

"That was then, this is now."

"So ...you were trying to come on to me?"

"I don't know," Sam said as he stared down at the floor, feigning fascination with the bar mat. "Chad, I have feelings for you, but we've been friends for so long it's hard to know if the two things are separate or not. I don't know what I'm feeling."

Chad leaned against the counter and ran his hand across the back of his neck, attempting to relieve the tension brought on by the revelation. "Well, I'm here if you want to talk about it, but I need you to come to terms with who you are. And what you want your life to look like before you pull another stunt like tonight."

"I just need some time to figure things out."

"Sure, take your time. Look, I'm wiped after the whole first-day thing. I'll see you at school tomorrow." Chad clapped Sam on the back and headed off to his suite, closing the door.

Sam ran his hand over his face, wiping away the tears that had finally sprung free and headed up the stairs.

Chapter Thirteen | March

The light snow that had fallen overnight was sticking, but the sun was out, and Gus had convinced everyone to go outside for lunch and throw a ball around.

"What the hell are we doing out here?" Dillon shouted as he took off running across the field with the football, ready to launch it to Tyler as soon as he was in position. "I'm freezing my nads off."

"Good, because assholes like you shouldn't be allowed to procreate anyway," Gus said, snorting.

"Oh, Augustus used a word with more than two syllables. Awesome effort," Dillon said. "There may be hope for you yet." He tossed the ball to Gus and deeked around Tyler, heading for the protection of the rest of the group. "Come on guys," he said to Chad and Sam. "Let's get this game going before I freeze to death."

"I'm going to sit this one out." Chad reached into his pocket, pulled out some rolling papers and a bag of weed.

"Yeah, me too." Sam dug around in his lunch pulling out the sandwich and discarding it under the tree. "Besides, my ass is frozen to the ground. I couldn't get up if I tried."

"Fine, suit yourselves." Dillon turned and flew back across the field to try to intercept the pass that Gus had just made to Tyler.

Chad set his binder on his lap and laid the papers out before carefully sprinkling in the amount of weed he was looking to wrap, then tucked the bag back in his pocket and deftly rolled the joint.

He lifted it up, turned to Sam and ran his tongue seductively down its length to seal it, and then winked at him.

"Fuck off, Chad," Sam said.

"What? Simply rolling a joint over here."

"I don't need you busting my balls over this."

"What about sucking on your balls? Would that work for you?"

Sam had to clench his teeth to keep from exploding.

"Chad," he said. "I'm going to kick your ass if you keep this up."

"You're no fun at all, you know that? Here ..." Chad passed Sam the joint and pulled a lighter out of his pocket. After he lit it, Chad waited for Sam to take a drag before taking it back. "So, where are you on the gay acceptance scale?"

"I'm not sure." Sam took the joint back from Chad and leaned heavily against the tree they were sitting under.

"Anything I can do to help?" Chad nudged Sam and smiled deviously at him. He laughed as a look of anxiety crossed Sam's face. "I'm kidding. Man, you're really not having any fun with this at all, are you?"

"Not when you're the one ribbing me, no." Sam passed the joint back to Chad and rose to his feet. "I'm going to head in. It's too fucking cold out here. Are you coming with me?" He stared nervously at Chad. "I'm heading to the locker room to warm up."

"Really?" Chad extinguished the joint and brushed his hands on his pants. "Are you sure?"

"No, but I want to find out. Are you coming or not?"

"Yeah. Sure." Chad gathered up his things and waited while Sam told the guys they were headed in to do homework. He followed him down the hall and into the gym, making sure to stick to the walls to avoid the security cameras that were meant to keep people out of the locker room, but anyone that had ever bought drugs on school property knew precisely where the cameras were aimed. Once they were in the locker room, Chad threw his backpack down on one of the benches and approached Sam who was watching him anxiously.

"Are you sure you want to be doing this with me?" Chad asked.

"Chad, I've wanted it to be you for years." Sam dropped his gaze shyly and shook his head. "Watching you at practice …and then in the showers …" He tucked his arms around his waist, hugging his body. "God …the number of times I've wanted to kiss you …"

"Why didn't you tell me?" Chad put his hand on Sam's chest and pushed him back across the room until Sam was pressed up against the wall.

"You're my best friend. I didn't want to lose you."

"You wouldn't have lost me." Chad brushed his hand along Sam's cheek and held his chin, thumbing his bottom lip. "You're too important to me." He lowered his mouth onto Sam's, gentle and soft, and felt an unexpected surge of emotion. He increased the pressure and pulled Sam to him as he ran his hands over Sam's firm body. He grabbed onto Sam's hips and pulled him closer still, and shivered as he felt Sam's stiffening response pressing against his thigh. His breath was shaky as he pulled away and studied Sam's eyes.

"Sam, no offense, but I wasn't expecting that."

"You felt it too?"

"Like a fucking earthquake." Chad retook Sam's mouth, diving deeper. He pulled away breathing heavily. "Fuck. Are you cool with going all the way?"

"With you ...yeah."

"Damn it, Sam. I could fuck you right here."

Sam shook his head, looking around. The bell would be ringing again soon, and there was sure to be a gym class.

"Not happening," he said. "We need to go somewhere else."

Chad groaned. "I'll be lucky to make it as far as my car, but I think we should head for the parking lot at the beach. No one is there at this time of year."

Sam swallowed a jumble of anxiety as the magnitude of what was happening or going to happen, flooded through him.

Chad layered himself up against Sam's body again and aggressively took his mouth, shattering them both.

"Fucking hell," he gasped, "that's unbelievable. Are you sure you're all right with this?"

"This is just between you and me, right?" Sam replied. "I'm exploring new things here, and I don't want the guys to find out."

Then he pulled away.

"I don't know," Sam said. "Maybe it's too weird that we're even contemplating doing this."

"Sam, if you don't want to do this with me, I'm all right with it."

Chad lifted Sam's hand to his mouth and took Sam's thumb into his mouth, playing it lightly with his tongue. He moaned softly as he began sucking on it, savoring it.

Sam's breathing shuddered, prompting Chad to drop Sam's hand and move closer. He pressed their bodies together, exhaling seductively against Sam's neck as he allowed his hand to drift down Sam's body. Sam inhaled sharply as Chad's hand descended lower, gripping, and rubbing him through his jeans.

"But, I think you'd regret your decision," Chad said then groaned as he grabbed Sam's ass, dragging him closer.

"I need you to fuck me," Chad whispered, tickling Sam's ear with his tongue and grinding hard against him. "I need to feel you deep inside me—hard. So damn hard …"

Sam shuddered against the wall, need and desire replacing the anxiety. "Fucking hell, Chad," he whispered. "This is a side of you I didn't know existed."

"Sam, come play in my world, and I'll show you all sorts of things you don't know about me."

It was well past the end of lunch hour, and the temperature was starting to drop as the sun began its descent. The leather of the backseat felt extremely cold against Chad's bare chest, and he wanted to lift himself off it. He reached back and wrapped his hand in Sam's hair one last time, and then rolled himself over, so he was facing him.

"I think we should throw a parade," Chad said.

"I hate to ask," Sam replied. "Why?"

"It would be a 'Sam finally lost his virginity' parade."

"Fuck off." Sam pushed himself up and moved Chad's legs out of the way, so he could sit down. "These seats are fucking cold."

"That's the downside of leather seats, unfortunately. The upside being that they're easy to clean." Chad looked around at the state of the backseat, laughing. "Which is definitely going to be necessary. Thanks for helping me christen the car."

"Can you stop with the jokes for two seconds?"

"I'm serious. Can you throw me those paper towels from under the driver's seat?" Chad took the roll off Sam, tore off a few sheets and began wiping up the mess they'd made.

"How can you be so casual about this?" Sam asked.

"Sam, it's just jizz. Chill out, would you."

"Not that. The sex. It was my first time—ever."

"You're right. I'm sorry." Chad stopped what he was doing and set himself to listen. Sam deserved that from him. "So, was it what you expected? Totally weird? What?"

Sam grinned. "At the risk of making you even cockier than you already are …it was amazing. More than what I expected."

"And I wasn't even trying." Chad laughed when Sam shoved him. "Now, if you'd bought me dinner first …"

"See. I knew you'd be an asshole about this."

Chad leaned back into the seat. "No, seriously, Sam." He reached out and ran his fingers along Sam's jawline, ending at his chin. "It *was* pretty amazing. I'd like to keep hanging with you, recreationally. If that's all right with you."

"No strings attached?"

"Strictly playtime. I'm not looking for a relationship."

"I'm definitely in on that," Sam said as he began rooting around for his clothes. "But right now I'm freezing. Hand me my pants, would you? We have some time before we need to pick Dillon up at school. Do you want to grab a burger or something?"

"You seriously want Dillon riding in the backseat before I've cleaned it properly?" Chad laughed loudly as Sam made a face. "Let's head over to my house. We'll have someone clean the car, and we'll have a few hours to ourselves before the guys show up. I'm sure Tyler will give Dillon a ride."

Sam sighed, nodding, then smiled.

"All those libido jokes," he said, "and remarks about your insatiable appetite are about to bite me in the ass, aren't they?"

Chad grinned. "You have no idea, baby."

Sam exhaled loudly, fell back onto the bed beside Chad and hauled the blanket up to cover his body.

"I'm exhausted," he said. "Chad, you're a maniac."

"We'll have to start you on a course of vitamins or something."

"This is so much better than the car." Sam shifted his body so he could tuck into Chad's shoulder and lay his arm on Chad's chest.

"Yeah, no chafing …and no frostbite." Chad played his fingers over Sam's hand.

"What time is it anyway?" Sam rolled over and grabbed his phone off the bedside table. "Fuck, it's already four thirty." He tossed it back and stretched out under the covers.

"Didn't anyone ever tell you time flies when boys play."

"No, I can honestly say I've never heard that one." Sam closed his eyes to rest for a minute and groaned when Chad dove beneath the blankets. "Don't you ever get tired, libido boy?" He gasped and gripped onto Chad's shoulders as Chad began dancing his tongue across his stomach and onto his hip, nipping at it.

"Do you want me to get tired?" Chad asked from beneath the blankets.

"Not if you keep doing …that, right there. Damn, Chad, where did you learn to do all this stuff?" Sam moaned and then fell instantly silent, gripping the covers; he'd heard someone enter the sitting area of Chad's suite.

He reached for Chad and tapped his shoulder.

Dillon had crossed the sitting room and was standing outside Chad's bedroom door, listening carefully.

"Chad, are you all right?" he asked. "Someone told me you weren't at school this afternoon?" He knocked once, then opened the door.

At the sound of the door opening, Chad shot up from beneath the covers and flew to his side of the bed, while Sam ducked into the warmth beneath the covers where Chad had been. But as Dillon stepped into the room, Chad gave Sam a hard shove with his feet, pushing him off the far edge of the bed onto the floor, out of sight.

"Hey, Dillon." Chad scrambled to cover himself up with a sheet, unsuccessfully; the covers had been pulled off the bed with Sam.

"Fuck, I'm sorry," Dillon said, shielding his eyes. "I didn't know you had someone in here with you." He kept his eyes averted until Chad grabbed a pillow to cover himself.

"Not your fault. I should've locked the door. Can you give us a few minutes ...to finish up?"

"Sure thing. But have you seen Sam? I couldn't find him at school. And you left early. I don't know where he is."

"I dropped him at his house earlier. He wasn't feeling well." Chad adjusted the pillow in his lap. "Dillon. I'll be out in a few minutes." He smiled and nodded until Dillon got the hint and left the room, then scrambled over to the edge of the bed and peered over, laughing at the state of Sam sprawled out on the floor.

"You think this is funny?" Sam reached up, grabbed onto Chad and hauled him onto the floor, knocking over the bedside table and the lamp that had been on it. He cleared the broken lamp out of the way and threw Chad over the fallen table, coming up close behind him, and breathing heavily in his ear.

"What are you going to do now?" Chad asked as he arched his body seductively, brushing his back against Sam's chest, his ass across Sam's cock. "Was I a bad boy?"

Sam chuckled softly. "The worst." He bit at Chad's shoulder, growling with anticipation. "You are in *so* much trouble."

The bell rang, and Sam checked the time on his phone before heading to the washroom in the east wing of the school. He threw his backpack up onto the counter and pretended to be washing his hands as the last of the students left to head to class. He pulled his phone out again and read the text that Chad had just sent him, laughing to himself as he thought about how their friends would react if they read it by accident. Chad was rude on his best days, but when he was all fired up, he was disgusting.

Sam smiled and sent Chad back a message that would make him hustle. He was getting tired of waiting for him. They'd been seeing each other *recreationally* for three weeks now, and Chad was always looking for new and exciting ways to meet up with him. The busiest school washroom during class time was the latest of his hair-brained ideas.

Chad came bursting through the door, tossing his backpack aside and grabbed onto Sam's shirt before hauling him into a cubicle. He slammed the door shut and pressed

Sam against the wall, desperately attacking his mouth. He pulled back, breathing heavily as he spoke into the curve of Sam's neck.

"Interesting text," he said.

"You liked that, hey?"

"Is that something you want to try sometime?" Chad ran his hands up Sam's chest and around the back of his neck as he looked into his eyes. "Because I'm game."

"Maybe." Sam shoved Chad hard against the far side of the cubicle causing the metal to rattle. "But you have to do something for me first." Grabbing onto Chad's belt with a rough hand, he yanked the buckle loose and smiled as he saw the glint appear in Chad's eyes, followed by Sam's body being spun around to face the wall. Sam gripped the edge of the cubicle as Chad struggled with his jeans, and wrenched them off his hips.

Chad sunk to his knees behind Sam, gripping the cheeks of his ass, and grinned as a "Fuck yeah," escaped Sam's lips.

They ran off down the hallway in separate directions, already twenty-five minutes late for class. Sam slipped quietly into the math class he had with Dillon and waved his apology to the teacher as he dropped into his seat.

"Where the fuck were you?" Dillon asked, doing his best to whisper under his breath, but the girl in front of them turned around and *shushed* him.

"I had a bit of a rendezvous to go to." Sam kept his eyes on the teacher and the board, speaking from underneath his cupped hand.

"No way. With who?"

Dillon was shushed again, and this time the teacher took notice.

"Is there a problem back there?" the teacher asked.

"No, sir. I was just asking what I missed." Sam pretended to be examining Dillon's notes, of which there turned out to be none.

"Come see me after school today, and we'll discuss it."

Sam sighed and started writing down the formulas that were on the board, and then discreetly opened a piece of paper that Dillon had passed to him. It simply read, *Who?* Sam flipped it over and wrote, *Someone really hot! And I mean fucking sexy, set my balls on fire, hot!* And handed it back. He jumped when Dillon kicked his chair and glared at him. He tore another piece of paper from his binder and wrote, *Not telling.*

He almost laughed aloud when he heard Dillon snort in disgust beside him.

When the bell rang for lunch, Sam made a point of sprinting ahead of Dillon as they made a run for their regular spot outside. He arrived first and came crashing down onto the ground under the tree beside Chad, almost knocking him over.

"What's the hurry?" Chad asked, shielding himself as Dillon flew at Sam and pinned him to the ground.

"Who is it?" Dillon asked. "I can't believe you're not going to tell me." He held Sam down and started smacking him in the head playfully. "Come on. We've been friends since kindergarten."

"I'm not telling," Sam shrieked, laughing.

"Telling what?" Gus arrived and stood a distance away from Sam and Dillon who were now wrestling each other for dominance.

"Sam was twenty-five minutes late for class today because he had a rendezvous." Dillon smacked Sam hard across the head. "And he won't tell me who it was with."

"What's a rondu ...what?" Gus scratched his head and sat down.

"A meeting. Usually of a sexual nature." Chad took a bite of his sandwich. "Maybe he's too embarrassed to tell us who it is." He poked Sam hard in the ribs. "Was it fast and hot?"

"Totally." Sam pushed Dillon off and reached for his lunch.

"How hot?" Chad tried to look disinterested in the answer.

"Scorching. But I don't think I'd want to do it again."

"Why not?" Dillon stretched out on his back, staring up into the new leaves that were opening on the tree.

"I think I'd prefer something more personal. Maybe even gentle." Sam looked straight at Chad and made eye contact before dropping his gaze and redirecting his attention to his lunch.

"That doesn't sound like much fun." Dillon pulled himself up and caught the football Gus tossed up to him.

"No, I think Sam has a point," Chad said. "Especially if the other person is someone really important to you." He winked at Sam then leaped onto his feet and took off across the field to catch the ball Dillon had already launched.

Chad moved around his room lighting a multitude of candles before he put on some music, shut the blinds, and locked his door. The guys had just left for the night, but they were known to return unannounced on occasion, and that was the last thing they needed.

"Who knew you were such a girl?" Chad said.

"Don't be an asshole about this?" Sam pulled his shirt off over his head and threw it onto a chair.

"No, I wasn't trying to be. I like it." Chad ran his fingers across Sam's lips. "I think it's sweet."

"Sweet?"

"Is that a bad thing?" Chad finished undressing Sam and turned to his own clothes before leading Sam over to the bed.

"Um …I'm not sure." Sam climbed under the blankets, surprised when Chad gathered him up in his arms to hold him. He'd never initiated that before, ever.

"It's not," Chad said. "There's nothing wrong with a bit of soft, gentle, and sweet every once in a while." He kissed Sam carefully on the forehead. "It can fuck with your emotions a little though."

"I've heard that." Sam paused. "Was it like that between you and Derek?"

"Yeah …" Chad sighed, brushing his cheek against Sam's hair. "Derek wasn't much of a *rough and tumble* guy."

"And you were all right with that?"

"Of course. Why wouldn't I be?" Chad turned and gazed upon Sam's face, studying his expression. "We don't have to do that other stuff anymore if you don't want to. I think we've moved past the whole *recreational sex* thing anyway."

Sam blinked.

"So, what would that make this?" he asked.

"Are you comfortable with being my boyfriend?" Chad brushed his fingers along Sam's face. "I'd really like you to be."

"Yeah ...I'd like that." Sam rolled onto his back and stared at the ceiling. "Who could've imagined that someday we'd end up here. Together in bed, talking about being boyfriends?"

"I'm glad we are, Sam ...and I'm glad it's you. You really are my best friend, in every way." Chad lifted his body and came to rest on Sam's chest. "One gentle and sweet coming right up, boyfriend."

Sam laughed then sighed as Chad gently took his mouth.

Chapter Fourteen | April

Chad was looking forward to the events about to play out. Zeek, Marlboro, and Pete were all coming back to school today after being cleared of suspicion in Derek's disappearance. When he'd heard the news they were returning, there'd only been one thing on his mind. He'd arrived in his English classroom early, expecting, and craving the confrontation. Luckily, Mr. White wasn't there yet, and Zeek was—and he was waiting for Chad.

"Hey, faggot," Zeek said. "Where's your girlfriend? Oh, I forgot. He's probably dead at the side of the road somewhere." He surged toward Chad, aggressive, leering, and laughing at him.

"You're a disgusting excuse for a human being," Chad said. "What is your problem with gays anyway?" He stepped up in Zeek's face, grinning. "I think I know exactly what it is." He stepped back slightly to brace himself. "It's like that line from Hamlet.... *The lady doth protest too much*."

He winked knowingly at Zeek. "You like fucking boys, don't you, Zeek?"

That's all it took to set Zeek off. He ran at Chad, knocking him to the ground, and drove his fist into Chad's face, then grabbed his head and began bashing it against the floor.

Chad could feel the world start to spin and he tried to maintain consciousness as Zeek continued to abuse his face. He only had to hold out until Mr. White arrived. As the seconds passed, Chad struggled to cover his face with his arms and protect himself from Zeek's fists; he was starting to have difficulty breathing past the blood now filling his mouth. He groaned in acceptance as he heard Marlboro enter the room and begin his own string of obscenities.

He felt the first kick from Marlboro's heavy boots land in his ribs, and he cried out, choking on the blood that was making its way into his lungs. When he felt Marlboro's boot make contact with his head, Chad reached out for Derek in his mind, picturing his beautiful face. He wanted Derek's image to be the last thing he remembered if he died. His mind began to dim.

I'm coming, baby...

Chad groaned when the muffled sounds of Mr. White and the school's police liaison officer running into the room brought him back. Within seconds, Zeek and Marlboro were handcuffed and led from the room. They likely wouldn't be coming back to the school ever again. They'd be punished for all the hateful things they'd ever said or done to Derek. In Chad's mind, it was well worth the pain he was in, and it would've been worth dying for.

Chad's hospital room had been a flurry of activity for a couple of hours, but it was starting to calm down with Sam and Dillon being the only remaining visitors. Chad was sitting upright in bed, attempting to hold a melting ice pack to his face.

"Dillon," Chad said. "Could you get me another one of these ice packs from the nursing station?" He pulled it away from his face and cringed. "This damn eye is swelling up again."

"Sure thing," Dillon replied as he grabbed the old one and headed out the door. As soon as he was partway down the hall, Sam let out the breath he'd been holding for days and collapsed against Chad's bedside.

"What the hell were you thinking?" Sam asked through shattered breaths. "Provoking them to go after you like that?" He gripped onto Chad's arm. "You almost died, Chad. They almost killed you."

Chad dropped his head.

"That was the plan," he whispered.

"What?" Sam shouted then spun away from the bed. "Fuck your fucking plan! You've been in a coma for days." He wiped viciously at the tears that were rushing down his face. "I thought you were never going to wake up."

"Hey." Chad reached for Sam's hand, directing him back to the bed. "Please don't cry."

"I almost lost you." Sam gripped onto Chad's hand tightly. "Are there any other stupid plans I should be aware of?"

"I still have to deal with Pete when I get back."

"No fucking way." Sam pulled away and began pacing around the room furiously. "We'll take care of Pete. I can easily get his locker combination if I hack into the school's computer, and Tyler has enough blow kicking around, thanks to your *mad money* canister, that he won't mind giving some up for the cause. We can get Pete done up on some pretty hefty drug trafficking charges."

Chad nodded. "Thanks, man. I appreciate it."

"Why did you do it, Chad?"

"You know exactly why I did it."

"But the police said the guys had nothing to do with what happened to Derek."

"Just because they didn't have anything to do with Derek's disappearance doesn't mean they wouldn't have done it if they'd been given half a chance."

"You're fucking obsessed." Sam sunk against the edge of the bed. "You almost died for him."

"I would've done it for any of you guys."

"Jeez, Chad." Sam relaxed. "What am I going to do with you?"

"Anything you want, boyfriend." Chad beamed at Sam and checked the hall for Dillon. "How are you holding up through all this?"

"Like crap. You really are a jackass, you know that?"

"That's what you keep telling me, so it must be true." Chad laughed as he grasped Sam's chin and brought him down for a kiss.

After being released, Sam placed his forehead against Chad's.

"Chad, I honestly don't know what I would do without you."

"You'd be just fine, remember." Chad looked up, pulling his hand away from Sam's arm. "Hey, Dillon …" He reached for the ice pack. "Thanks, buddy."

Sam moved away from the bed and pretended to be checking his cell phone for text messages. "Dillon, I'm going to hang out with Chad for a bit longer. You have that big makeup test in math tomorrow, so you don't need to stick around. I'll take a taxi home."

"Yeah. Jeez, I hate math," Dillon said. "See you later, guys."

"Just memorize those notes I gave you and you'll be fine." Sam pounded Dillon on the back and waved to him as he left the room. He waited and checked the hall before he closed the door, and then climbed up on the bed, carefully lying down beside Chad. It was already late and well past visiting hours. They should be safe enough to spend some time together, just them, in each other's arms. Sam knew he needed it. To feel Chad, alive, in his arms.

"Mm …this is nice." Chad cuddled into Sam's chest.

Sam gently stroked Chad's face, taking special care over the areas with the stitches and bruises. "They really did a number on your face, didn't they?"

"You should see the rest of me. I almost puked when I saw myself in the mirror."

"I'll check it out in a week or so." Sam settled a soft kiss on the top of Chad's head. "I meant what I said earlier."

"About me being a jackass. Yeah, we covered that already."

"No. About being without you. I couldn't...."

Chad burrowed tighter against Sam, hugging him close.

"Sam, you're my best friend," he said, "among other things. I wouldn't want to be without you either."

"It's gone beyond that for me." Sam pulled himself away so he could look into Chad's eyes. "I think I'm in love with you."

"Jeez, Sam." Chad sighed and cupped Sam's face in his hand. "I don't know what to say. I have strong feelings for you too. Way beyond friendship, but—"

"You don't have to feel the same way. I just wanted to tell you how I felt." Sam settled a soft kiss on Chad's lips. "Now you know." He shifted down in the bed so he could share Chad's pillow, and maybe get some sleep. Chad closed his eyes and listened to the comforting rise and fall of Sam's breath, and realized it was a sound that he could easily listen to for the rest of his life. He tucked himself in and let the sound lull him to sleep.

Evelyn had been on her way home, after dropping off a few of the boys after their visit with Chad, when she'd decided to head back to the hospital. Her son had been in a coma for days, and the doctors hadn't been certain as to whether or not he was going to fully recover. She wanted to sit by his bedside and just watch him sleep for a while before going home, knowing that when morning came, he'd wake up the same as anyone else.

She made her way quietly down the hall and past the nurse's station. There was no one there, which was a relief because visiting hours were over. Although they had been extremely lenient with her when they'd first brought Chad up to the wing.

Evelyn remembered the call she'd received a few days ago from the hospital. Her heart had almost stopped when the doctor told her, her son had been beaten badly at school and was currently unresponsive. She and her husband had raced to the hospital, and they'd sat by his bedside in shifts, waiting for him to wake up.

Chad had finally awoken early that morning, flooding her with waves of absolute relief when he'd smiled at her and started into a normal conversation with her.

She pushed the door open and set her coat and purse down on the chair by the door. She made her way over to the bed, quietly, so as not to wake him up, and was extremely surprised to see Sam curled up, cradling her son in his arms. A tear rolled down her cheek as she watched them sleep. Sam and Chad had been best friends since they were young children, but she'd had no idea how deep that ran. Her husband had made a good choice in picking Sam to be Chad's associate within the firm.

She took a seat over in the corner of the room and decided to close her eyes for a while. She'd wake Sam up in an hour or so and give him a ride home. She heard them stirring, but then they quietened, so she didn't bother getting up. She couldn't really see them from where she was sitting, but she assumed they'd probably gone back to sleep. She closed her eyes again, and they started speaking quietly to each other. Not wanting to intrude and being curious as to what two teenage boys could possibly have to say to each other under the current circumstances, she kept silent.

"Hey, I didn't think you'd still be here," Chad said.

"I'm not going anywhere until they kick me out."

"Thanks for staying. I like it when you hold me." Chad turned onto his side and kissed Sam gently on the lips. "Mm …and you always taste so good."

"Jeez, Chad. I love you so much."

"That makes me hot when you say that."

"Everything makes you hot." Sam laughed softly. "I love you." He kissed Chad ever so carefully. "I love you. I love you."

At this point, Evelyn wished she'd made her presence known as soon as they'd woken up. It was possible she was misinterpreting what was being said, but that was extremely unlikely at this point. The whispers of love had turned into sounds of something much more physical.

Evelyn comforted herself with the fact that Chad was definitely feeling better before she cleared her throat.

"Fuck, Mom!" Chad said, sitting up. "What the hell are you doing here?"

"I came to watch you sleep, but apparently you don't have sleep on your mind." Evelyn stood and straightened out her clothing as best she could, and fussed with her hair while Chad rearranged himself in bed. "So, boys. When did this happen?"

"About two months ago," Chad said.

"I wasn't aware that Sam was …"

"Gay? Yeah, he came to a bit of a realization a few years back, but didn't get up the nerve to tell me until …February?"

"Yeah, it was February," Sam said.

"I told him to think about it a bit more before he jumped into anything. And he did." Chad tucked himself down on the pillow and reached out for Sam's hand. "I didn't expect there to be anything between us, but when we shared that first kiss …it was like freakin' fireworks going off."

"We've been sneaking around ever since." Sam shifted Chad back onto his chest. "The guys don't know about us."

"I don't know what to say," Evelyn said.

"Just be happy for us, Mom."

"I am, sweetheart. But it's going to be quite an adjustment seeing the two of you together like this."

Chad smiled at his mom. She really was the best.

"Thanks, Mom," he said. "I knew you'd be cool with it. Sam's parents, on the other hand, are not going to be as accepting."

"We'll work on that together," Evelyn said as she approached the bed and gave each of them a kiss on the head. "The doctor says you can go home tomorrow if you get a good night's sleep and he feels you're up to it." She snapped her fingers. "So, Sam, I'm giving you a lift home. No arguments."

"Yes, Mrs. Parker," Sam replied, hauling himself off the bed. There really was no point in arguing. Like Chad, Chad's mom always got exactly what she wanted.

Chad was released from the hospital the next day, as anticipated, to the care of his mom, who brought him home and set him up on his sofa with a blanket, a cup of tea, and the television clicker. The pain medication, although welcome, made his mind a bit foggy, but Chad brightened as soon as he heard his friends spilling down the stairs.

"So, what kind of stuff have they got you on?" Tyler asked as he sat down beside Chad, looked him directly in the eyes, and started laughing. "That's some good shit. Your eyes are all fucked up."

"Nice, Tyler. Thanks," Chad said.

"I guess that means you're not allowed to drink," Gus said as he started pulling beer and chips out of a bag.

"I'll have some of those chips," Chad said. "I've got serious munchies, and my mom just keeps giving me tea." He made a feeble attempt to catch the bag of chips that Gus threw to him.

Dillon picked them up off the floor and opened the bag for him.

"I hear pot is good for pain." Dillon dug around in his jacket looking for the metal container he kept his rolled joints in.

"I'm pretty sure it shouldn't be mixed with prescription pain meds. Might be overkill." Chad stuffed a handful of chips into his mouth and then motioned for Sam to bring him a cola from the fridge. "Thanks. Too many chips, not enough liquid." He tracked Sam with his eyes as he brought the can over and sat down beside him.

"How are you feeling?" Sam asked as he discreetly slid his hand under the blanket and brought it to rest on Chad's leg.

"Much better now that all you guys are here." Chad smiled at each of his friends in turn. "So, what are we going to watch? I'm up for some straight porn if it'll keep you guys around for a long visit."

"You're like our best gay friend ever." Tyler flicked on the television and headed straight for a porn channel.

"He's our only gay friend, asshole." Gus pushed Tyler over and took control of the clicker, turning up the volume to get the full effect through the surround sound.

Chad laughed, groaning and swearing under his breath as the movement hurt his ribs. He pretended to be massaging them as he slipped his hand under the blanket, and took Sam's hand.

Sam shuffled closer to Chad once the guys were fully engrossed in the action on the screen, smiling up at Chad when he felt Chad squeeze his hand affectionately. He turned his head to listen as Chad leaned in toward him.

"I love you too, Sam."

Chad beamed as an incredible flush of color rose in Sam's face.

Chapter Fifteen | May

The bell had rung fifteen minutes ago, and Sam was hanging out at Chad's locker waiting for him. Chad was running late, as usual, and the guy with the locker next to Chad's was becoming annoyed at the fact Sam was there every day after school. He opened his locker door and let it bang into Sam's shoulder.

"Watch it." Sam pushed the locker hard in the other direction and was caught off guard when the guy pulled him away from the lockers and pinned him to the wall across the hall.

"Hey, leave him alone!" Chad ran down the hallway and pulled the guy off Sam. "Don't be hauling my friend around."

"Friend? The way he looks at you every day when you finally get here? I think you have a new boyfriend. Faggot."

"Who are you calling a faggot?" Sam jumped up in the guy's face, making him back down. "Go ahead. Say it again."

Chad stepped in between them, shoving the guy onto the floor.

"You better fuck off before I bust your head," he said, glaring at the guy as he pulled himself up and took off down the hallway.

Chad turned to Sam, checking that the hallway was empty.

"Sam, I don't think you should wait for me here anymore. I'll have a set of car keys made up for you. You can wait for me in the car after school." He waited while some students passed by the doorway at the end of the hallway before pushing Sam up against the lockers.

He played with the front of Sam's shirt and leaned in close to him. "And you've got to stop making those damn puppy dog eyes at me. People are starting to notice, and it makes me so fucking hot. It's distracting."

"You know I can't help it." Sam grabbed onto Chad's belt, pulling him closer, and checked up and down the hall before bringing him to his mouth. The sound of the doors at the end of the hallway crashing open and their friends running toward them didn't register until it was too late.

Chad pulled away and cleared his throat before pushing Sam out of his way and opening his locker. He pretended to be looking for something at the bottom of it for a few seconds until he could compose himself. By the time he straightened up and closed his locker, Dillon, Gus, and Tyler were standing across the hall staring at them in disbelief.

"When were you going to tell us about …whatever this is?" Dillon asked, his voice rough with disdain, as he waved his hand at them. Then he leaned against the wall, the anger visibly building behind his eyes.

"We weren't." Sam shrugged his shoulders and stuffed his hands into his pockets. "Not yet anyway."

"You fucking bastard!" Dillon advanced on Chad, shaking with rage, and shoved him hard into the lockers. "Sam's been your best friend since grade two for fuck's sake. How did you manage to pull him into something like this with you?"

"I didn't pull him into anything!" Chad pushed Dillon back across the hall then drove his fist into the lockers behind him. "Thanks a lot, *friend*. What kind of deviant fuck do you think I am anyway?"

"Dillon, he didn't. It was my idea. I came on to him." Sam made to approach Dillon, but Dillon backed away from him.

"Since when are you gay?" Tyler screwed up his face and threw his backpack onto the floor. "Fuck man! We went camping together last week. You were sleeping right beside me."

"Fuck off, Tyler!" Sam said, spinning angrily on his heel. "I wasn't going to make a move on you."

"You just said you made a move on him, didn't you?"

"Yeah, but Chad is gay, and I like him …that way."

"I feel sick." Gus sank down onto the floor and wrapped his arms over his head. "You guys aren't …you know. Are you?"

"Jeez, Gus. How long have you known me?" Chad said, his voice rising in frustration. "Do you really need to ask that? Of course, I'm fucking him." He threw his hands up in exasperation when Sam glared at him. "What? I'm not about to sugar coat it."

"You're an asshole, you know that?" Sam grabbed his backpack from the floor and started for the doors. "I'll be in the car. I have my own set of keys."

"Sam," Chad called, watching Sam disappear through the door.

"In the car, sweet stuff," Sam shouted over his shoulder.

Tyler's hands found their way into his hair. "Holy fuck."

"How long has this been going on?" Dillon crossed his arms and leaned back against the wall, glaring at Chad, but the hurt was starting to seep in around the edges of his eyes.

"We started up at the beginning of March," Chad replied.

"The day I walked in on you in your bedroom—" Dillon shouted as his eyes flew open. "That was Sam in bed with you?" He ran his hand through his hair as Chad nodded. "We were all sitting out in the lounge! We could fucking hear you!"

"I feel really sick." Gus began to rock back and forth against the wall, prompting Tyler to squat down beside him and pass him something that Chad was sure wasn't an aspirin.

"I'm sorry," Chad said. "I wasn't thinking."

"And the *fucking hot* rendezvous of Sam's that I found out later was in the guy's washroom. That was you?" Dillon asked.

Chad nodded. "Yeah, that was me."

"So this has been going on under our noses for almost three months, and you weren't going to tell us ...yet?" Dillon looked like he was on the verge of tears. He crossed his arms even tighter across his body. "When? When were you going to tell us?"

"We figured we'd get bored of each other after a while and then you guys would never have to find out."

"And now what?" Tyler looked up from Gus' side.

Chad shrugged. "We're not bored."

"Fuck, Chad. That's not what I meant," Tyler said. "I want to know what happens now that we know."

"I'd love to say that if our relationship freaks you out …we'd stop, but we can't stop. It's moved beyond that."

"You're fucking kidding me." Tyler stood up. "If you tell me the two of you are in love, I'm going to hurl."

"Fine. I have to go. Sam's waiting for me." Chad made to leave but turned back again. "Are you guys coming over tomorrow?"

"No way," Dillon said. "I need some time to work this through in my head." He grabbed his backpack and headed for a different door from the one Chad was moving toward.

"Yeah, us too," Tyler said as he pulled Gus to his feet and followed the direction that Dillon had taken.

Chad stormed out into the parking lot and threw open the door of his car. He chucked his backpack into the backseat and dropped down behind the wheel. "Fucking morons!" He pounded the steering wheel with his palms then turned the engine over.

"I take it the rest of the conversation didn't go well," Sam said. "Nice job on the *fucking me* part by the way. It was a very classy touch. Way to win them over."

"Shut the fuck up, Sam. If I'd wanted a nagging girlfriend, I'd have picked up one of those bitches from the cheerleading squad."

"Why are you mad at me?"

"Because it was your stupid idea to start sleeping together."

"I didn't hear you complaining. A lot of moaning and groaning, and *harder Sam*, but no complaining."

"Jeez, Sam, if I didn't love you so much, I'd pitch you out on your ass right now and make you walk home."

"Lucky me. I get to sit in the car with you all the way home instead." Sam stroked a hand down Chad's arm and smiled at him.

Chad turned in his seat, brushing a thumb across Sam's chin. "I'm sorry for being such an ass. You know I love you."

"I love you too, jackass." Sam settled back in his seat. "Now, take me home. I need a drink after all that fucking drama."

Chad backed out of Dillon's driveway and stopped at the bottom after being told by Dillon's mom that Dillon wouldn't need a ride to school with him anymore. He'd been up and down that driveway a thousand times or more. Running and cycling as a small child, and now that they were old enough, driving. He'd even brought one of the horses up there more than a few times. He pulled away and drove a few more doors down to pick up Sam.

"Where's Dillon?" Sam slipped into his seat and threw his backpack into the backseat.

"He doesn't need a ride from us anymore. According to his mother, Dillon is uncomfortable being in our company." Chad looked over at Sam, who'd dropped his head onto his chest. "He'll come around eventually."

"He's our best friend. I don't understand how he could just dump us like that." Sam pulled out his phone and texted him. "Tyler and Gus. Maybe. But Dillon?" He looked down when his phone beeped.

"What did he say?"

"Essentially to fuck off and die, but more vividly put."

"Tyler and Gus both texted me the same thing this morning."

"I guess it's just you and me then." Sam smoothed his hand onto Chad's thigh and smiled over at him. "And I'm all right with that."

"Yeah, me too." Chad pulled the car over to the side of the road and turned to face Sam. "We've got another month of high school together, and after that, we're going to university together, and after that, we're going to be working together. That's a lot of together."

"Does that scare you?"

"No." Chad reached for Sam's arm to reassure him. "Quite the opposite actually."

"Good, because I feel much better knowing you'll be there with me going through all those changes. You've been a constant force in my life since I was eight."

"That is kind of cool, isn't it?" Chad shifted in his seat. "This is going to seem strange and really old fashioned, and I'm not really sure what it'll look like, but ...I don't just want to be your boyfriend. I'm obviously not talking about getting married or anything, but I'd like us to be somewhere in between."

"Chad. I know you take our relationship seriously." Sam squeezed the hand that had found its way into his. "Where we are doesn't need to have a name or a ring attached to it. We love each other, and we're going to be spending a hell of a lot of time together. Let's just leave it at that for now."

"I just wanted to let you know where my head's at."

"I appreciate that."

Chad pulled the car back onto the road and took in the views of the lake. There was so little wind; the water took on the illusion of a perfectly reflective surface. The constant force was standing still for a moment in time and allowing the fleeting images to be reflected as if it was watching them for a change. He grasped onto Sam's hand and brought to his lips, not wanting to waste any of the time he'd been given to enjoy him.

Chapter Sixteen | June

The hotel's grand ballroom with its massive windows overlooking the lake was decorated with elegant dashes of black, white and silver, and a small band had begun playing some cover music to start out the evening. The main entertainer would be making an appearance a few hours later. The graduates had started arriving in droves as the sun started to set, but Chad and Sam were still sitting outside in their limo.

"Are you sure you want to do this?" Sam asked as he pulled at Chad's tie, trying to get it to sit right. Satisfied, he brushed a few stray hairs off his shoulders. "No one knows about us. We could escape from high school relatively unscathed if we leave now."

"But then they won't have learned anything about the way they treated him ...treated us."

"Derek again—" Sam slumped back in his seat. "How is it that *everything* always comes back to him?"

"Because I learned a lot from him in the short time I knew him." Chad leaned forward in his seat to put his point across. "Most of the students at this school judged Derek before they even got to know him. He was written off as *that gay guy*. He was so much more than that. The whole practice of stuffing people into little boxes and closing the lids—it has to end. We're real people too, and we have as much right to love as anyone else. We shouldn't have to hide away to keep the hateful people happy. I'm not prepared to give them that much power."

"But look what happened to Derek?"

"We don't know for sure what happened to Derek. If it was a hate crime …that's all the more reason for us to keep pushing back. They can't win this."

"All right," Sam sighed. He couldn't win this either. "Let's do it for Derek then."

Sam kissed Chad and climbed out of the car. He waited for Chad, and then took his hand as they crossed the parking lot to the hotel entrance. He found the entire experience of walking past the other students with their hands clasped extremely stressful until he realized he'd never felt more at peace with himself than he did at that moment, the love of his life at his side.

They approached the check-in table and signed their names before proceeding toward the ballroom entrance.

"Do you want to do the picture thing?" Chad looked over to where other couples were getting their pictures taken under the school's graduation banner.

"I think we'd be pushing it," Sam replied then grinned. "Plus, those pictures are hideous."

"Agreed." Chad interlaced his fingers tighter in Sam's and led him into the ballroom. It was fairly dark in there, but a few people immediately noticed they were holding hands.

"Let's go find a table," Sam said, peering around for one. "Preferably not anywhere near our team—" His breath caught. "Never mind, they've spotted us."

"What do you want to do? Hold? Not hold?" Chad asked, looking over at Sam, trying to gauge his level of anxiety.

"Hold—don't you dare let go of me."

Sam held fast and watched as a couple of the members of their team, including the team captain, Lou, started across the dance floor toward them. He momentarily panicked when Chad dropped his hand, but then recovered when Chad placed an arm around his waist and pulled him close.

"I want to be able to catch you if you pass out on me," Chad whispered so close to Sam's ear that Sam could feel Chad's warm, comforting breath roll across his neck, making him laugh.

"Hey, Chad. Sam," Lou said as he stepped up to them. "You guys look great."

"Thanks, Lou. You're looking good yourself." Chad looked around at the people staring at them. "We're a bit late. Did we miss anything exciting?"

Lou laughed. "Other than a gay guy showing up with his date that no one knew was a gay guy ...nope."

"Damn. And we missed that?" Chad clapped Lou on the shoulder and shook his hand. "Thanks, man. I appreciate it."

"Anytime. Are you guys going to sit with us?"

"No, I think the plan is to cruise around here for a little bit and then head home."

Lou clapped his hands together, laughing.

"Just making an appearance like a couple of rock stars," he said.

"Something like that. We're actually leaving early tomorrow morning for the university. My dad has us signed up to do some volunteer work over the summer."

"So, this is it then?"

Chad shrugged. "Yeah, we're out of here after this."

"Well, it was a pleasure playing ball with you." Lou shook Chad's hand and then turned to Sam. "And you, sir ...full of surprises, aren't you? It was a pleasure." He shook Sam's hand and then turned to his group of guys to herd them back across the floor.

Sam looked past them toward the grouping of tables Lou and the rest of the team were headed for.

"Dillon, Gus, and Tyler are sitting over there," he said.

"I know. I see them." Chad made eye contact and nodded to each one of them. Every one of them looked away.

"I think we should go home and finish packing," Sam said, taking Chad's hand and bringing it to his lips.

"Yeah. There's nothing for us here."

Chad wrapped his arm around Sam's shoulders and pulled him close, giving him a kiss on the cheek.

"Mm ..." Sam sighed. "Let's go."

Chapter Seventeen | Six Years Later

The deciduous trees surrounding the main concourse of the university, frantic with masses of first-year bodies as they tried to find their way around the campus, rustled briskly in the breeze, multitudes of brightly colored leaves waving back and forth, appearing to be saying goodbye to summer.

Chad and Sam, leaning against the perimeter wall, watched the chaos, laughing as they saw the same people going around in circles. This was to be their final year at the university, and they were looking forward to finishing up and getting out into the real world, master's degrees in hand.

"So, our final year," Sam said. "And they're finally letting us share a room."

"I'll be glad to get out of the regular dorms. Those first years are crazy ass stupid. It'll be nice to get a good night's sleep."

Grabbing their bags, they headed to the quarters allocated for the students in their final year of their master's degrees and laughed as they saw the size and amenities of their new room.

"Fucking awesome." Sam dropped his bags and high fived Chad. "This is what I'm talking about. No more sneaking around during the night."

"Help me push these beds together."

"Later. Let's crack the bubbly." Sam hauled a couple of bottles of champagne from his bag and two plastic cups. He filled both and passed one to Chad. "Here's to our final year in university, and to the future, when we can finally get our hands on a few hotels."

"Cheers to that."

Chad finished his third glass of champagne then climbed onto the bed by the window and flopped down on it. Sam lay down beside him, joining him in staring at the ceiling.

"Are those swirls moving?" Chad asked, blinking.

"That is very possible." Sam sat up and filled Chad's glass, plus his own, and took a deep breath. "Chad …question?"

"Sure, what is it?"

"What are your views on marriage?"

"What were you thinking?" Chad sat up, set his glass on the floor, and took Sam's hand in his.

"I was thinking that once we finish here and move to Vancouver, we should get married. We've been together for more than six years, and I can't imagine being with anyone else."

"Yeah, I know what you mean." Chad cradled Sam's face and kissed his lips. "I just …I just don't know."

Sam pulled away. He knew that look in Chad's eyes.

"Fuck, Chad!" he shouted. "Is this about Derek again?"

Sam flew off the bed, pacing angrily around the room. "When the hell are you going to let him go? They never found him! He's fucking gone, Chad! Gone!"

Chad shook his head.

"No," he said. "I'd know if he was really gone. I'd feel it."

Sam backed further away from Chad. This was never going to end. Derek would always be with them, alive or not.

"No, you wouldn't," he said. "You're not joined together by some fucking cosmic chain of some sort."

"Sam …"

"No. I can't believe you're still on about this. Do you really love me? Or am I just a convenient second?"

"Sam, please. I love you …but you know I'll never be able to forget Derek completely. I'm sorry …please." Chad stood and crossed the room to take both of Sam's hands in his. "I want to marry you. I do. Will you marry me?"

Sam sighed and smiled begrudgingly at Chad.

"Yeah …I will," he said. "I'll marry you …you stupid jackass."

Winter break arrived, and Chad and Sam decided to spend it in Vancouver going over the wedding plans with Evelyn and buying a condo for when they moved there in June. Sam had insisted he didn't want to live in one of the hotels where their suite wouldn't have a proper kitchen. He didn't like dining out all the time and wanted to be able to have frequent home-cooked meals.

In reality, his mother had instilled a love of baking in him that had been severely stifled during his time at university, and he was anxious to get back into it.

Chad hadn't been able to stop laughing when Sam had meticulously checked out the oven in the new condo and then ordered a completely different one.

"Who knew you were such a homebody," Chad said.

"It's important for it to feel like a home," Sam said as he stood in the middle of the living room, glancing around at the stark concrete walls of the penthouse suite. "Although, I don't know how that's going to be possible in this place."

"I thought you liked this one. Did you want the penthouse in the other building? You liked the layout better than this one. But I thought you wanted a view of the ocean."

"No, I love seeing the ocean. And I like that it's two stories like this. And the balconies are breathtaking. But it's so …"

"It's not big enough." Chad leaned against the wall. "We can keep looking and have this one for when people visit."

"Chad—" Sam laughed. "I'm pretty sure five thousand square feet will be plenty of space for the two of us to bump around in."

He paced the expansive living room and took in the views beyond, and then headed back to the kitchen.

"There's just so much glass," he whispered mostly to himself.

"Wait until the decorators get in here. You'll see. Once they get the floor to ceiling draperies up …you'll notice a big difference."

"I'm entrusting your mother implicitly to do this place up." Sam finished putting the last of the glasses into the cupboard and started in on the silverware. "Did you pick these out or did I?" He turned each piece over and examined it before placing it in the drawer.

"My mom did. She didn't like the ones you'd picked out."

"So what they say about mothers-in-law may be true after all."

"She loves us and just wants our first place to be perfect."

"I know. I don't mind actually. I'm especially glad she's taken over the wedding arrangements." Sam closed the drawer and leaned against the counter before pulling Chad to him. "I'm excited."

Chad kissed him, pressing his body closer.

"Me too," he said. "It just seems right, doesn't it? Marrying your best friend. You probably know me better than I know myself."

"I know everything about you. And I love you anyway."

"Thanks a lot." Chad snuck a quick kiss onto Sam's cheek and then lifted the empty box off the counter and threw it onto the floor with the rest of them. "I love these marble countertops." He brushed his hand across the surface. "They're kind of cold though."

"That's the downside of marble countertops, unfortunately," Sam said. "The upside being that they're easy to clean." He grinned at Chad, remembering their first time together in the backseat of Chad's car. It took a second for the reference to register, but when it did, the gleam in Chad's eyes set Sam's heart racing.

Chapter Eighteen | Monday

The valets showed up early at the university by private jet on the morning of graduation and headed straight for Chad and Sam's dorm room. They began packing up their things before the men even had a chance to get out of bed. There wasn't much stuff, but Chad had wanted everything put away in their penthouse before they arrived home, so their valets had made an additional trip.

"Do you think they'll leave us any clothes to wear?" Sam watched the valets for a minute then rolled back into Chad's arms.

"I wouldn't worry about them." Chad kissed Sam's forehead and tucked him tighter against his chest as he observed the flurry of activity. He sat up, pushing Sam aside. "Hey, Todd! Hold up a minute." He patted Sam's hip. "I think I spoke too soon."

Chad leaped out of bed and crossed the floor to talk to Sam's valet. After a five-second conversation, he flew back onto the bed.

"What was that about?" Sam lifted the blankets to let Chad crawl back in and gave him a puzzled look when he set a small velvet box down on his pillow.

"Open it," Chad said.

"You didn't. You did?" Sam popped open the box and pulled out the two rings that were inside. "Which one is mine?"

"Read the inscriptions."

Sam read the inscription inside each ring, shaking his head as a tear escaped. He brushed his arm across his eyes and laughed.

"Look at what you've done to me," he said. "I'm crying like a fucking girl."

"What do you think?"

"It's a beautiful sentiment." Sam passed his ring to Chad and held out his hand. Once his ring was on, he slipped Chad's onto his finger. "I guess we're officially engaged now." He sunk into Chad's arms, basking in the kiss that sealed their promise.

"I love you, Sam." Chad stroked the edge of Sam's ear, tucking a strand of hair behind it. "I really do."

"I love you too, baby."

"Hey, I was wondering." Chad paused. "Are you going to be taking my last name? It came up yesterday when I was talking to my lawyers about the prenuptial agreement."

"I hadn't really given it any thought."

"You've still got time to think about it. But I'd like you to."

"Samuel Parker." Sam closed his eyes. "Yeah, I like the sound of that." He looked up at Chad. "I'd love to."

Chad beamed at him. "You're amazing, you know that?" He kissed the ring on Sam's finger, gazing into his eyes. "I can't imagine being happier than I am when I'm with you."

"You have no idea how happy that makes me to hear you say that." Sam snuggled into Chad's side and watched the valets make quick work of packing up their room.

The graduation ceremony was long and tedious, but Chad was experiencing such a massive sense of relief for managing to complete his schooling that he wasn't really paying attention. It had been a struggle to stay focused, especially while at Tekla.

Even when he'd moved halfway across the country to attend university with Sam, he'd still found himself fighting against an overwhelming urge to just pack it in and go home.

He would've given it all up to have Derek back in his arms. He dropped his head, picturing him, and looked up again, smiling when he saw Sam approaching.

"Are you getting all sentimental about leaving this place?" Sam said as he stopped beside him.

"No, I was just thinking about how much I'm looking forward to getting back to the coast."

"Well, the car is waiting for us." Sam grabbed onto Chad's hand, led him away from the university concourse toward the limo, and away to their new home …and their new life together.

The penthouse looked more amazing than what Sam had thought possible. He walked through the entire space and secretly praised Evelyn for picking up on his need for touches of a traditional home. She'd managed to bring a cozy feeling to the massive, glass, concrete, and steel space.

"So, what do you think?" Chad asked, taking it all in. "Is my mom a genius with interior design or what?"

"It's amazing," Sam replied as he ran his hand over a hand woven wall hanging on the way back to the kitchen. "Did you check out my new oven?"

Chad smirked.

"No," he said. "I must've missed it somehow."

"Fuck off." Sam stroked his hand across the oven's sleek edge. "You'll be wishing you hadn't bugged me about it when I'm eating gorgeous baked goods, and not sharing any with you."

"Speaking of gorgeous baked goods ...my mom says she wants us to pick out some clothes for our honeymoon."

"Was that a reference to your mom or our wedding cake?"

"Very funny. I'm working through a list of things to be picked up. And I was thinking ...since I'm the expert in fashion thanks to my mother, I will take on the responsibility of honeymoon shopper. There are a few really nice shops not far from here. I'll check them out after work tomorrow and book a private shopping appointment at one of them."

"A private appointment?" Sam laughed. "You are definitely your mother's son."

Chapter Nineteen | Tuesday

It was getting late by the time Chad managed to get away from work. He headed toward the area that he was sure contained the store he was looking for. It would be bittersweet going into this particular store. It was one of his mother's favorites, *Taylors*, but it was also the same chain that Derek had worked for back home.

He took a deep breath, pulled the door open, and strode directly to the back looking for the manager. A slim young woman, who looked like she'd just stepped off the runway, approached him.

"Can I help you?" she asked.

"I'd like to speak to the manager."

"The manager isn't here right now. But I'm sure I can help you."

Chad stuffed his hands into his pockets as he looked around. "I'm Chad Parker. Carl Parker's son. We own a few of the hotels in town here. Maybe you've heard of him."

"Of course. It's a pleasure to meet you." She smiled and batted her eyelashes provocatively at him. "What can I help you with?"

"Yeah, um …my fiancé and I require some private shopping time with a consultant. We'd like to come in tomorrow around six."

"We usually don't close until nine, but we'll certainly close early for you and your fiancé when you get here."

"Thanks." Chad nodded his head. "I'll just scan around before I go." He was about to turn away when the impulse overtook him.

"You wouldn't happen to have someone named Derek working here, would you?" he asked.

"Oh sure. Derek is one of our managers. He works here two nights a week plus Saturdays. Did you want me to leave him a message? He just stepped out for a few minutes. You could wait for him if you like."

"No!" Chad felt his heart drop. "No, I ...please don't tell him I was here." He turned away from the clerk, gripping clothes racks to steady his retreat. As he exited the store into the foot traffic, the world took on a surreal pulsating and foggy quality. He contemplated the possibility of whether or not it was *his* Derek, as he wandered in the direction he hoped was the way back home.

He slowed to a stop, peering up, he was relieved to see he'd made it to their building. He looked to his valet, who'd been waiting for him to return, for assistance in making his way upstairs in the elevator. As the elevator door opened, Chad stumbled into the foyer of their penthouse and threw his coat onto a chair before making his way to the sofa in the living room.

"Chad? Are you all right?" Sam squatted down to look up into Chad's face as he sat down. "Let me get you a drink."

"Sure, yeah ..."

"What's going on? You look like hell."

"...nothing."

Sam poured a scotch and returned to sit beside Chad, and began rubbing his back. "Did you find a decent store?"

"Mm ...hm. Just down the road a bit. They'll work out fine."

"When is the appointment?"

"Tomorrow at six. But I have to go back there tonight. I forgot to tell them something."

"Can't you just phone the store?" Sam held the back of his hand to Chad's forehead, checking for a temperature.

"No, I have to see him in person."

"Him, who?"

"The manager."

"All right," Sam replied, nodding. "I'll come with you. I could use the walk."

"No, you can't do that!" Chad turned and looked at Sam anxiously. "I've arranged a surprise for you."

"Mm ...I like your surprises." Sam kissed Chad on the cheek and headed to the kitchen to finish making dinner. He had everything on the table by eight, which seemed to annoy Chad for some reason. He sat back and watched as Chad frantically picked through the food while continually checking his watch.

"Are you late for something?" Sam asked.

"I want to be back at the store before it closes."

"I don't see why you can't head over there in the morning."

Chad's head snapped up. "It has to be tonight!"

"Sorry. My mistake." Sam picked up his wine glass and leaned back in his chair. He'd never seen Chad acting like this before; he seemed to be on the verge of panic. "Is the whole wedding thing stressing you out?"

"No—" Chad stopped what he was doing, set his hands on the table, and looked across at Sam. "Why would you say that?"

"Because you look like you're ready to jump out of your skin."

"I've got a lot on my mind right now, that's all." Chad threw his napkin down on his plate and went to grab his coat.

"So, I'll see you in what …half an hour?" Sam shook his head when he heard the elevator door close, his question unanswered.

The walk back to the store seemed to take forever even though Chad was moving as fast as he could on legs that were taking on the consistency of jelly. Through each step, his mind kept telling him it was impossible. If Derek was alive and well, why hadn't he contacted him? It was just a coincidence.

He rounded the corner that would place him directly across the street from the store and stopped. His heart raced up into his throat as he turned to face the store. He held his breath as he scanned the interior. Fifteen minutes passed before he saw a door at the rear of the store open.

His breath caught, and he just about crumpled to the ground when he saw Derek step out.

His Derek.

Chad watched Derek chat with a few of the staff members on his way to the front door, tracking him as he stepped out onto the street. He was at a loss as to what to do next, so he kept pace with Derek, staying on his side of the street a block back. He had to run to catch up when Derek turned left away from him, racing across the street, almost being hit by a passing car before finding his way down the side street that Derek had taken.

He slowed as Derek approached a decrepit, old historic three-story walk up and pulled out a set of keys. Within seconds, Derek was inside, and the door swung closed.

Chad moved into the vestibule of the building and leaned against the wall, fighting to stay conscious. He sunk to the ground and held his hands over his face, scrubbing away the tears that were running down his cheeks as he tried to catch his breath.

The world he'd been living in suddenly seemed inconsequential as he pulled himself to his feet. He approached the door and ran his hand down the directory until he found the nameplate that listed a 'D. Sugar - 323' and he froze.

Derek had changed his last name.

Maybe he didn't want to be found.

He sunk down onto the steps and cried, rocking himself against the wall, prompting a few passersby to stop and ask if he was all right before moving on. Thirty minutes passed before he wiped the tears from his face, took a deep breath, and stood, firmly pushed the button. It rang twice before it was picked up.

"Hello?" the voice said.

"Derek?" Chad's heart thundered away inside his chest as he waited for a response. It was definitely *his* Derek. He would recognize that soft, beautiful voice anywhere.

The door buzzer echoed in the small vestibule, signaling the door was unlocked for him to enter. Chad stepped into the building and made his way up the stairs to the third floor, and turned toward apartment '323'. The hallway took on a strange hue of color and motion, forcing Chad to support himself against the wall as he crept toward the door. He gripped the doorframe as he slipped the engagement ring off his finger and stuffed it into his pocket. He tapped lightly on the worn surface below the number.

Derek had returned home and checked for phone messages before going to the bedroom to strip off his work clothes and put on his favorite kimono. He'd flicked through a few channels on the television and was about to make some tea when his phone rang for the front door. It was late. He'd almost not answered.

The voice that had come through the handset had almost caused him to collapse. It shook him to his core.

Derek placed his hand on the lock, pausing for a second to gather himself. But there was no stilling the hammering of his heart.

He took a deep breath and opened the door.

Chad took one look at Derek and fell crashing to his knees, bowing his head, and began to sob uncontrollably.

"God, Chad ..." Derek's legs buckled at the sight of the man kneeling before him, and he sunk to the floor, falling into Chad's arms; as strong and comforting as what he remembered.

"Chad, please don't," he said. "Not for me."

Chad sat back, taking Derek's face into his hands and kissed his lips, lingering over the taste of them.

"Derek, I—" he started, but Derek shook his head, laid a tender kiss on Chad's lips and pulled him to his feet, into his apartment.

Standing just inside the door, Chad traced the outline of Derek's face with his fingers, as he sought out the differences and then ran them through the soft curls of Derek's hair.

"I missed you so much," he said.

Derek pushed the door closed and tucked his face into the curve of Chad's neck, kissing him just below his ear.

"I missed you too," he whispered.

Chad shuddered beneath his touch, releasing a new stream of tears. They found their way onto Derek's cheek, throat, and then his kimono. He crushed Chad closer to him. Never wanting to let go.

"Derek, what happened to you?" Chad asked.

"Not now. I'll tell you. But not now." Derek brushed his hand through Chad's hair then wrapped his arms around Chad's body. "Right now, I just need you to hold me." He stroked his cheek against Chad's chest as Chad's embrace enveloped him. "I never had the chance to tell you how much I loved you."

"Derek—"

"I never stopped loving you. Not for one second."

Chad buried his face in Derek's hair, inhaling the scent of him. He'd awoken to that scent for weeks after Derek's disappearance, clutching Derek's sweater to his face as he slept all those years ago.

"God, Derek," he said. "I love you too ...so much."

Derek looked up with soft, wet eyes. "You do?"

"From the first day I set eyes on you." Chad brushed his lips across the crest of Derek's forehead and kissed a path down the bridge of his nose. "Not a day has gone by that I haven't thought of you."

Derek dropped his gaze, stroking his hands down Chad's chest, fidgeting with the buttons. Chad's hands found his, encouraging him to unbutton them, and the shirt slipped easily from Chad's body. Derek whispered a soft kiss onto Chad's skin just above his hammering heart, encouraging a groan as he encircled Chad's body.

They undressed each other in silence, stroking hands over skin they'd each been longing for, and sunk down onto the floor, their bodies moving in perfect unison, rising and falling to each other's rhythms. Their mouths met in a fury of endless emotion as they held each other, and cried for the night they'd missed so many years before, and all the years they'd been apart.

Derek wiped the tears from his face and curled himself up on the sofa by Chad's side, tucking his body tightly against him, and resting his head on Chad's chest.

"We looked for you," Chad said as he gazed down into Derek's face. "Everyone thought you'd been killed."

"I know." Derek's body began to shake, and he grabbed Chad's hand to hold against his face. "I'm so sorry. But after what happened to me, I didn't think you'd want me back."

Chad pulled back ...after what had happened?

"Derek," he said. "You're all I've ever wanted. I've been living my life waiting for you to come back to me."

Derek peered up into Chad's eyes. "You have?"

"I thought I was going to die when you went missing."

"God, Chad—" A shudder shook through Derek's body, reducing him to tears again, prompting Chad to tuck Derek even tighter against him. He lay his face against Derek's hair, breathing in the familiar and comforting scent of him.

"Shh ...baby." Chad set his lips against the top of Derek's head. "Tell me what happened."

"My dad—"

Chad pulled away, staring at Derek. "What?"

"My dad was waiting for me when I got off work. I thought he'd come to apologize. Ask me to come home, but ..."

"Fuck, no—" Chad cradled Derek's head to his chest.

"He said he wanted to talk. So, I went to sit with him in his car."

Derek squirmed against Chad's body.

"I don't remember much after that," he continued. "He offered me something to drink ...iced tea I think." He closed his eyes and buried his face in Chad's chest. "I do remember him calling me a *fucking queer prostitute*, but my head started to get really foggy. I think he must've drugged me."

Chad's body tightened, and he cringed, holding his breath, but he didn't interrupt. He needed to hear everything.

"When I woke up, I didn't know where I was. And it was dark. I remember feeling really cold and wet." Derek brushed his fingers through the hair on Chad's chest, fanning it toward his neck. "I was outside, behind a building ...probably an alley. This guy came up to me, asking if I needed any help. I told him I needed to find a phone." He raised his eyes to meet Chad's. "I was going to phone you to come get me."

"Why didn't you? I would've come for you."

Derek tucked his head back down. "Never got the chance. The guy—Paul. He told me he had a phone in his place two blocks over. I followed him ...all stupid and naïve." He interlaced his fingers with Chad's and squeezed tight. "I spent the next two years with him."

Chad shifted. "I don't understand."

Derek looked back up, holding Chad's attention. "I belonged to him, Chad. He essentially owned me. I was his *boy*." He dropped his gaze back down, slipping his hand out of Chad's. "I got so I would do anything for him. If I didn't, he would get so angry ...hold back on the drugs I'd become so dependent on."

Derek shook his head remembering.

"Drugs he'd hooked me on," he whispered. "But if I kept him happy, did what I was told ..." Derek paused, closing his eyes. "Earned him money ...he was really good to me."

Chad's body shook, grief coursing through his body. He'd known Derek was alive, and deep down he'd also known Derek was suffering. "What did you have to do ...to earn ..."

Derek cupped his mouth, breathing into it, slowing the dizziness and nausea rising in his throat.

"Chad," he said. "This is tough stuff for me to talk about."

"Derek, I love you." Chad turned Derek's face up and kissed him, then tucked Derek back against his chest. "I won't judge you. Nothing you tell me will change the way I feel about you."

Derek exhaled slowly through his nose. "I did quite a few videos for Paul, for this website he runs. Sometimes by myself. Sometimes with other guys. Made a lot of friends actually. But part of the attraction of the site was an unwritten bonus that you could *date* the models ...for a price. I was very popular."

"Fuck." Chad scrubbed a hand across his face and pinched the bridge of his nose, attempting to stop the tears. "Why didn't you call me? I would've come. Even after that ...I would've come."

"Deep down, I think I knew that. But I couldn't bring myself to call you. I didn't want you to see me like that." Derek set a simple kiss on Chad's lips to keep him from speaking. "I know what you're going to say, and believe me, you wouldn't have wanted anything to do with me. I was a strung out hustler that eventually got dumped back on the streets when Paul got bored with me. I stayed there, feeding my habit by going on dates until I ended up in the hospital one too many times." He leaned back into the sofa, crossing his arms. "I decided to clean myself up. I finished high school, took a few business courses, and started working at *Taylors* just a few blocks from here. I'm the assistant manager there now. Just like we talked about."

"I know." Chad smiled, pulling Derek back into his arms and kissing his cheek. "I was at your store today, setting up a private appointment for tomorrow. That's how I found you."

"Really?" Derek's face lit up. "I think that's why I applied at the same store I worked for back home. Deep down, I was hoping you'd come looking for me someday."

"It would've been easier if you'd just called me."

"Yes, but there was no guarantee your phone would actually be turned on." Derek shrieked and clung to Chad as Chad's hands scooped him closer, tickling him. He caught his breath and looked over at the coffee table. "Speaking of which. My phone has been going off furiously for the past ten minutes."

Derek reached over, grabbed his phone and read the text, then turned to look at Chad. He reached for Chad's left hand, but not finding anything, he rubbed his thumb over the vacant space.

"When are you getting married?" Derek asked.

"Next week." Chad reset his position on the sofa to face Derek.

"Why didn't you say anything?"

"Because it doesn't matter anymore."

"I hardly think that's true." Derek removed himself and headed to the kitchen to put the kettle on. He finished filling it and turned the burner on before rooting around in one of the cupboards looking for the herbal tea that he'd seen Chad drinking at his house.

Chad took the opportunity to look around the apartment. The best word to describe it was eclectic. There were colorfully beaded curtains on most of the doorways, and the furniture looked as if it had been transported from the nineteen sixties. And it was spotless.

He watched Derek moving about the kitchen in his pink kimono and smiled, as Derek turned and caught him staring.

"You still look good in pink," Chad said.

"Someone told me once that it brought out my gorgeous skin tone." Derek winked at Chad and grabbed the kettle, filled the teacups and carried them over to the coffee table.

"Chamomile, right?" he asked.

"Yeah, thanks."

"Don't you think your fiancé will be upset if he finds out you were out fucking an ex-boyfriend a week before your wedding?"

"Derek, that's not what we were doing."

"So …what?" Derek eyed Chad. "You're just going to blow him off. Just like that."

"I don't know, all right?"

Derek tucked himself up on the sofa and cuddled back into Chad's side. "I don't like this."

Chad reached for his jeans to retrieve his phone; it had started ringing. He reluctantly answered it. "Hey, what's up?"

"Where are you?" Sam asked. "I was expecting you home hours ago. I've been calling and leaving messages."

"I'm at a friend's place."

"We just moved here. Who could you possibly know already?"

"It's an old friend. Look. I'll be home soon."

"Who is it?"

"Don't worry about it, Sam. I'll be—"

Derek sat up in shock, and mouthed, "You're marrying Sam?"

Chad nodded his head, *yes*. Then ran his hand down Derek's face. As his fingers passed over Derek's lips, he shook his head, *no*.

"Chad, are you still there?" Sam asked.

"Sam, we need to talk."

"Why? What's going on? You were acting so strange all through dinner. Are you sure this isn't about the wedding?"

"No, it wasn't about the wedding. But now it is." Chad took a deep breath. "Sam, I found him."

"Found who?" Sam paused ...then exhaled, his breath faltering.

"Damn it, Chad," he whispered.

"I'm with him right now. I'm going to stay at his place for a few days. Maybe longer." Chad wiped a few tears off Derek's face, relieved, as Derek nodded, *yes*, and laid a soft kiss in his palm.

"I'm at a loss here," Sam replied. "You actually found him."

"Yeah, I did."

"So, are you moving in with him? Is that what's happening?"

"Just until we figure things out." Chad waited out the long silence, but Sam wasn't responding. "Sam, I still love you."

"You could've fooled me." Sam stopped to compose himself, using the heel of his hand to clear the tears from his cheeks. "What do you want me to do about the wedding? Is this going to delay things, or should I be canceling it altogether."

"Sam, just give me some time, all right?"

"You really are a jackass, you know that?" Sam sighed in resignation. Somewhere inside, he'd been expecting this.

"I'll delay the wedding for a month," he said. "If you haven't figured things out by then, I'm calling it quits. There's only so much pain I can handle, and you've put me through more than enough because of Derek over the years."

"Thanks, Sam."

"I should hate you right now." Sam held the phone tighter to his ear. "If I didn't love you so much, I would."

"You're my best friend, Sam. I really do love you."

"I know." Sam paused. "So, will I see you at work tomorrow?"

"Yeah, but I'll come by the penthouse first to pick up some clothes. I really am sorry, Sam."

"We'll talk more tomorrow."

Chad ended the call and ran a hand over his face, trying to clear the thoughts racing around in his head.

"So, you and Sam?" Derek asked, confused.

"Yeah. Turns out my best friend had a crush on me for years."

"You guys seemed so close. You didn't know he was gay?"

"Not a clue."

"Chad, are you sure you want to be doing this? You two sound like you really love each other. And you've got all that history."

"We do love each other. Sam means a lot to me, but it's not the same as how I feel about you."

Derek rubbed a clenched fist across his face, scowling. "But you only knew me for six days. You've known Sam for …" He stopped and counted the years back in his head. "Seventeen years. That's a long time. How long have you been seeing each other?"

"Since part way through second semester at Tekla."

"Oh, for fuck's sake, Chad! You can't do this to him."

Derek pushed himself away and went to sit on a chair across the room. He tucked his legs up and sipped on his tea as he thought about what Chad was proposing. He set his cup down.

"I love you, Chad," he said. "But this isn't right."

Chad leaned forward, setting his tea back on the coffee table, and rose to his feet.

"Sam has always known he'd come in second to you."

"What the hell does that mean?"

Derek leaped to his feet.

"He's been your best friend since you were eight years old," he shouted. "You're obviously in love with each other, and you've got a wedding planned for next week."

Derek scowled, charging forward toward Chad, prepared to shove him out the door.

"What the fuck are you doing here with me?" he shouted.

Chapter Twenty | Wednesday

It was seven in the morning by the time Chad worked up enough courage to head home to the penthouse. He knew the next few hours weren't going to be easy, and he'd actually considered phoning his mother for advice but had decided against it. This was his mess, and he was going to figure it out for himself.

Derek had set him up with a blanket and pillow on the sofa after their argument but had come out of his bedroom a few hours later to get him. Chad leaned against the wall of the elevator for support. They'd spent the rest of the night in each other's arms, whispering words of love and sharing stories of pain. Pain they'd both felt while they were apart.

Chad closed his eyes, remembering the exhilarating taste of Derek's skin and the soft sounds Derek had made as he'd explored his body. He took a deep breath to clear his head as the elevator door opened, and stepped into the penthouse. Sam was asleep on the sofa, the phone clutched tightly in his hand. He pulled out one of the bar stools and watched Sam sleep for a while. His heart tugged at him. He really loved Sam.

"Hey, Sam." Chad smiled as Sam's eyes blinked open.

"Hi. What time is it?" Sam pushed himself into a sitting position and took Chad's hand, pulling him down to sit beside him.

"It's almost seven thirty." Chad wrapped his arm around Sam and hugged him against his shoulder. "I'm so sorry for doing this to you. I had no idea …I mean, I suspected, but I had no idea how strongly I'd react to seeing Derek again."

Sam slumped forward, holding his head in his hands.

"So, where has he been all this time?"

"Here. In Vancouver. He changed his name though …to *Sugar* of all things."

"How did he end up here?"

"Sam …I really don't want to talk about this right now."

Sam looked over at Chad then straightened up, slapping his hands on his thighs.

"Oh, no you don't," he said. "We are going to talk about this. You phone me …out of the blue. Say things are off between us—"

"But, Sam, I don't know that yet. I just need some time."

Sam shook his head.

"Either way," he said. "You owe me."

"All right," Chad agreed. "You're right."

"Thank you," Sam said then reached for Chad's hand."

"How did you find him?" he asked. "Your dad's guys didn't have any luck, and they're supposed to know what they're doing."

"That's because they weren't looking in the obvious places. He's working for the same clothiers that he did back home."

"You're kidding. The place you made the appointment at?"

"Yeah. I asked the clerk on spec, and she confirmed it. I barely made it home. I thought my legs were going to give out."

"That's why you were acting so weird at dinner last night." Sam gripped tightly to Chad's hand. "How's he doing?"

"He's been through a lot of nasty stuff. He ended up doing porn, going on *dates*—" He gripped onto Sam's hand when he felt him pulling away. "And he got pretty heavy into drugs for a while. But he's got himself straightened out now."

Sam sat straight up, alarmed, searching Chad's face, unsure as to whether or not he wanted to know the answer. "You didn't have sex with him, did you?" He could see by Chad's eyes that he had. "Please tell me you used protection. He might have something."

"I wouldn't risk putting you in danger like that."

Sam pulled himself off the sofa and headed to the windows.

"I can't believe you cheated on me as easily as that," he said. "After everything we've been through together. All the times I've been there for you over the years, saving your ass. Does none of that mean anything to you?"

"I'm sorry, Sam. I couldn't stop myself. It was like completing a circle that has been floating over my head for years."

"So, now that the circle is complete, can we get back to our lives and move forward with the wedding?"

"It's not that easy."

"Why not?" Sam braced himself for the inevitable answer.

"We love each other. It wasn't just me. Derek's in love with me."

"How is that even possible?"

"I don't know. We must've connected on some whole other level."

Sam crossed his arms as his face twisted. "I'll tell you what, Chad. How about I don't postpone the wedding at all, and you and Derek get married instead. It'll confuse the hell out of the guests, but hey ..." His arms exploded from his chest. "It's Chad Parker! He can do whatever the fuck he wants!"

"Sam, stop."

"Stop? Fuck you!" Sam stormed from the room and up the stairs to the bedroom, slamming the door.

Chad dropped his head into his hands. The problem with having your best friend from childhood as your future husband was the tendency to tell him every detail of any situation. He should've kept most of what he'd told Sam to himself.

No. Sam was his best friend.

He deserved the truth.

Chad climbed the stairs and stepped into the bathroom as Sam started up the shower.

"Sam, I love you. But I can't move forward with you until I know where I stand with Derek."

"I know exactly where you stand with him." Sam stepped into the shower and started washing his hair. "It's the same place you've been standing since you thought you lost him. And from what you're telling me, he's been doing the same."

"I don't understand."

"You've both been standing firmly in each other's hearts." Sam shut off the water and opened the shower door. "Get in. We need to get ready for work, and I really need you to hold me."

"Damn it, Sam. I'm so sorry." Chad stripped off his clothes and stepped into the shower, taking Sam into his arms.

"Don't be sorry." Sam tucked his face in against Chad's cheek, stroking one hand up into Chad's hair to draw him closer, the other clinging to Chad's shoulder. "I wouldn't trade the time we've had together for anything in the world."

"Sam, please don't write us off yet. Just give me some time with Derek. Let us sort things out." Chad pulled away and cradled Sam's face, studying his eyes. "Will you wait for me?"

"I don't know that I have a choice. I love you too much to let you go, and I love you too much to hold on to you. Just, please …don't take too long." Sam ran his hands down Chad's face and kissed him softly. "I don't want to lose my best friend."

"You won't lose me—" Chad said, sealing the promise with a kiss. A promise he wasn't sure he could keep.

Chapter Twenty One | Thursday

The morning meeting had been brutally tedious. They'd started at eight in the morning, finally emerging after four hours with very little accomplished. Chad slumped off to Sam's office to rest his eyes and get a drink before the next meeting started at two thirty. His dad was chairing the afternoon meeting, which meant they'd actually get something done, hopefully.

"Please shoot me before we have to work with the marketing department again." Chad dropped his feet on Sam's desk, reclining in a chair with a drink in hand, as Sam took a seat across from him.

"Better yet," Sam replied. "Let's fire the marketing department and start fresh. Our most prestigious and modern hotel is in the middle of Yaletown, and they don't understand why we should be selling it as a destination for gay couples. They must be walking around with blinders on. Rainbow filtering blinders."

Chad laughed, swung his legs down off the desk, and walked around to stand beside Sam. He brushed a hand across Sam's shoulders, rubbing his back. "I love you, you know?"

Sam closed his eyes. "I know." He held his breath as Chad kissed his head and started for the door.

"I'm going to surprise Derek for lunch today. He starts work at two, so I'll see you back here after I drop him off."

"Sure thing, Chad." Sam slid deeper into his chair as Chad closed the door. Chad had stayed at Derek's two nights in a row now. That first morning, Chad had come back to the penthouse and made love to him, telling him how much he loved him. But Sam hadn't seen Chad this morning until he'd arrived at work. All he could do was wait, and it was killing him. He poured himself a drink and called his secretary to order him some lunch.

Chad balanced the totem pole of take-out food he'd picked up on the way to Derek's in one hand, as he attempted to work the key Derek had given him, in the lock. He breathed a sigh of relief when Derek opened the door for him. The relief quickly disappeared when Chad walked into the apartment and saw that Derek had company. He deposited the food in the kitchen and turned to face the obviously wealthy executive sitting at the table.

"Chad," Derek said. "This is Spencer. He comes to see me on Thursday, *every* week, from twelve until one." Derek circled around the table toward the kitchen to see what Chad had brought back with him. "Spencer, this is my boyfriend, Chad. Who will *not* be coming home for lunch on a Thursday ever again."

Derek smiled at Chad then dug into one of the Chinese takeaway containers. "Right, sweetheart?"

Chad was speechless.

He stared back out toward the table and gripped the counter, churning explanations around in his head as to why Derek would have a standing appointment with this man.

Spencer nodded at Chad. "Pleasure to meet you." He ducked his gaze. "Derek, I'm going to head back to work and let you have lunch with your boyfriend." He stood quickly from his chair, almost knocking it over and then blushed. "I'll see you next week? I really need to finish talking to you about that …thing."

"Of course, darling," Derek sang out in a voice that made Chad cringe. "I'll be all ears. I'm always here for you. You know that." Then Derek saw Spencer to the door, stepping out into the hallway for a few seconds before coming back into the apartment. He threw an envelope onto the coffee table, flopped down on the sofa, and continued eating his lunch.

Without looking up, he said, "Chad, come, sit. We need to have a little discussion."

"I assumed you weren't doing that anymore," Chad said as he sunk down on the sofa beside Derek, and just stared at him.

Derek shook his head and cleared some sweet and sour sauce from his lips with a napkin.

"You assumed wrong," he said. "They've become part of my routine. It's like being paid to have lunch with a friend and listen to their problems. Maybe comfort them a little."

"Do you have sex with them?"

"Sometimes. Most of them aren't looking for that though." Derek crunched up his eyes. "Maybe the occasional blow job." He clicked his chopsticks together, pointing toward the door. "Spencer there ...he sometimes needs that extra bit of attention. Especially when his wife is on his case. Or his teenage daughter is being bitchy." Derek laughed softly, picking through the noodles in the container. "Truthfully, he ends up in my bed at least twice a week, poor thing."

Derek waved his hand to dismiss everything, set his food down and headed to the kitchen to put the kettle on, but as he stood just out of Chad's sight, he fought to contain the tears threatening to escape, exposing his ruse.

He'd been thinking a lot about what Chad was willing to give up for him, and he just couldn't let him do it. He loved him too much. Chad belonged with Sam, the man that had always been there for Chad, and who now loved him; a man who Chad truly shared a life with. Their lives were so intertwined that pulling Chad away from one part of it would mean unraveling the whole thing, and Derek couldn't live with the consequences of that.

He'd been formulating a plan in his mind since that morning. He'd envisaged spending the weekend with Chad first though. He brushed a tear from the tip of his nose. Having Chad show up at lunch today, and seeing Spencer there, had provided him with a perfect opportunity to start the plan early. Spencer was actually the only client he still saw anymore, and he never wanted to do anything more than talk, but Chad wasn't going to know that.

Derek composed himself and returned to the living room.

"And before you get all freaky on me," he said. "As soon as you showed up at my door, I told my clients that sexual favors were off the table ...for now." He grabbed Chad's take away container off the coffee table and opened it. "Are you going to eat your lunch, or am I going to have to feed you?" He clicked the chopsticks together in Chad's face. "See. I'm an expert now."

Chad pushed Derek's hands away.

"I'm sorry," Chad said. "But I never imagined I'd meet one of the guys who's paid money to have sex with you." He covered his mouth, nausea shimmering up from his gut. "Fuck, Derek ..."

Derek brushed his fingers together, finishing off a spring roll.

"You make it sound so pedestrian," he said. "I'm not in the business of sex for money. It's more like a mutually beneficial companionship."

Chad choked out the next question. He needed to know.

"How many of these guys are there?" he asked.

"Well, let's see." Derek stopped, tapping a finger on his chin as he pretended to ponder the question. He'd already worked out the lie, calculating the severity required to crush Chad.

"I have a client every day from twelve until one, except on Sundays," he said. "I had to move my Saturday afternoon client to Friday because you and I will probably want to hang out on Saturday before I go to work. I have a couple of clients that like to take me out for dinner or to functions occasionally." He paused. "In total, there are probably ten men that I'd consider regulars. I can usually bring in an extra thousand a month."

Chad's head swam as he shook it in dismissal.

"You don't need to be doing that anymore," he said. "I've got more than enough money to buy you anything you want."

Derek jammed the chopsticks into the container. "I more than realize that, Chad. You tried to do that for me once before. Now, don't get me wrong. I'm not ungrateful for what you did ...and what you were trying to do. But I can take care of myself."

Chad set his expression, firm. This situation wasn't going to stand. He would not have Derek tricking himself out for cash.

"Derek," he said. "You're not doing this anymore."

Derek raised one eyebrow at him as he ate a mouthful of noodles. He set the box down on the table and went to check on the kettle. Once Derek was out of sight, he pretended to be fussing with the teapot while he furiously wiped away the tears that were leaving tracks on his cheeks. He leaned against the wall.

"Do you want tea?" Derek asked.

"No, thanks."

"All right." Derek checked his appearance in the shiny surface of the toaster, relieved to see the anguish wasn't showing on his face. He exhaled deeply, set his shoulders, and walked back into the living room. "Chad, you can't just walk into my life and start ordering me around. You don't get a say. This is my life."

"But, Derek—"

Derek set the teapot down firmly on the coffee table. "If you don't like it. There's the door." He sat down and crossed his legs, but then popped up again. "I think I hear my phone."

Chad turned in his seat, watching Derek race off into the bedroom, closing the door behind him. He heard the thud of Derek's body leaning against it after he'd closed it over.

Collapsing onto the edge of the bed, Derek held his hands over his face and tried not to hyperventilate as the emotions washed over him. He took a few deep breaths and shook it off, peeled himself off the bed and re-entered the living room.

"That's strange," he said. "I'm sure I heard it, but it's not in there anywhere." He dropped down onto the sofa and leaned over, flicking open a metal box on the coffee table, and pulled out a joint. He lit it, took a long drag, and held it out to Chad as he exhaled.

"No, I don't do that stuff anymore," Chad said.

"That's too bad. This is really nice stuff. My favorite really." He took another drag then pinched the end off and dropped it back in the box. "You didn't eat a thing."

"I'm not really that hungry." Chad pushed closer to Derek, grasping his chin, and kissed him. When he sat back, Chad searched Derek's eyes and was confused when Derek looked away.

"What's wrong?" Chad asked, at a loss as to why his acceptance of Derek's terms was being met by such coldness. I'm not asking you to change. I want you in my life."

Derek shrugged, close to tears again.

"But why?" he asked.

"Because I love you," Chad said.

Derek rolled his eyes, sunk behind the shield that had protected him for so many years, and donned his *working* face.

"You're far too sentimental," he said, his voice dropping into the familiar pattern—husky, sexy.

He winked at Chad.

"Now come here to *sugar*," he said as he pulled Chad toward him, undoing Chad's tie, and the buttons of his shirt, pushing him over on the sofa. "Let's see if we can make you feel better."

Chapter Twenty Two | Friday

The evening meeting had finished on time, which pleased Chad to no end because it meant he could get his weekend with Derek started. His schedule had been crazy, and it wasn't leaving them much time to reconnect. He'd tried to get some time off, but his dad had become furious at the suggestion.

He scrubbed at his face.

He hadn't been able to think of anything else. Staying up late with Derek, talking, making love ...waking up together.

Chad grabbed his raincoat from his office and made a run for the door before anyone found him anything else to do. He stepped out onto the street and opened his umbrella. The night air was refreshing, with the scent of the ocean making him feel exhilarated and optimistic about his future with Derek. The whole incident at lunch yesterday had worried him. Then, when he'd arrived at Derek's late last night, they'd made love a few times, but Derek hadn't been able to stop crying through most of it.

He quickened his pace.

Hopefully, the weekend together would straighten things out.

As he made his way up the stairs and approached Derek's apartment, a thin, poorly dressed man stepped out and closed Derek's apartment door, nodding to him as he passed. Chad paused to watch the man jog down the stairs before letting himself into Derek's apartment.

"Jeez, Jake. What did you forget now?" Derek sat cross-legged at his coffee table with his back to the door, and he was busily cutting lines of cocaine on a mirror. He threw the razor blade down, grabbed a straw, and snorted a line. As he ran his arm across his nose, he turned to face the door. "Fuck. Chad. Is it that time already? I haven't even started dinner yet. I'm sorry."

"I came straight from work." Chad dropped down onto the sofa and stared at Derek in disbelief. "I thought you gave this stuff up."

"Mostly yeah. Personal favorite though." Derek turned and snorted the other line before cleaning off the surface with a wet finger, rubbing the remnants into his gums.

"So," he said. "What did you want to do tonight?" He jumped up and headed to the kitchen, pulling some stuff out of the freezer to cook for dinner. He threw a few things down on the counter and almost collapsed when he caught sight of Chad's face in the reflection of the microwave. He clung to the edge of the counter, hoping to contain the sounds of pain and anguish aching to escape as his heart was torn in two.

"I think I should go." Chad stood and headed for the door, but Derek ran out of the kitchen and intercepted him.

"Hey, if the drugs bother you. I promise …as soon as I finish what I have left, I'll never do them again."

"Derek, you lied to me about the drug use."

"I did not. I never said I'd stopped doing drugs. You must've formulated that in your head because that's what you wanted the truth to be. I never said I stopped."

Chad narrowed his gaze, studying Derek.

"Why are you doing this?" he asked. "The men. The drugs. You're so much smarter than this. You deserve so much more—"

"Says the man with unlimited access to anything his heart desires," Derek interrupted. "You have no idea how the rest of us live. What we have to do to get by while you sit up there in your fucking castle with theaters, pools, bowling alleys, and way too many fucking fridges!"

"Derek, please stop." Chad pressed the heels of his hands up against his eyes, trying to hold back the tears before they spilled down his face. "I love you, and I want to be with you. You don't need to live like this. Please. Come home with me."

Derek crossed the room and started going through some small containers on his bookshelf until he found the one he was looking for. "Now you've got me all stressed out." He dumped the contents onto the mirror and started chopping at it with the razor blade.

"Derek stop!" Chad reached down to grab Derek's arm, but Derek swiped viciously at him with the razor blade.

"Fuck off!"

"Derek, please," Chad pleaded, then backed off, letting Derek go back to what he was doing.

"Just leave me the fuck alone. I don't know what I was thinking. Fucking delusional that's what I am. Stupid. Go home. I feel more comfortable down here among my own kind."

"What the fuck are you on about? Your own kind? Jeez, Derek. You belong with me."

"No. Sam belongs with you. Not me."

"But Derek, I love you."

Chad watched Derek lean over the mirror, but had to turn away as he snorted the line.

"Go home to him, Chad. Please." Derek closed his eyes, cringing as the door slammed behind Chad. He was gone. Derek collapsed onto the floor, waiting until he heard the building door close before he began to sob. His stomach heaved as he crawled across the floor to the bathroom to throw up. Resting his face against the cold porcelain, he replayed the events in his mind, letting his heart twist its way through to its final destruction.

Jake had played his part wonderfully. Bringing the drugs over and keeping a look out for Chad to cue him up, and being sure to run into him on the stairs. The cocaine had definitely been the final straw. He wiped at his lips. He needed to make a phone call. He only needed one more thing in place in case Chad decided to come back to him that night.

The elevator doors opened onto a space that felt like a real home. The smell of freshly baked bread wafted out of the kitchen, and he could hear Sam humming to himself as he worked.

Sam heard the elevator door close and came out of the kitchen, beaming when he saw it was Chad.

"Hey, stranger. You're just in time for dinner." Sam took Chad's coat and hung it up for him. "Can I get you a glass of wine?"

"Yes, please. Thanks, Sam."

"So, what happened to your big weekend with Derek?"

"I walked in on him doing lines of blow."

"What? I thought you said he gave all that stuff up."

"That's what I thought. Apparently, I was mistaken. He tried to lay the misunderstanding on me as if I'd come to that assumption out of need. I swear though, he deliberately left out information to lead me to that conclusion."

"I'm sorry, Chad."

"And yesterday when I went to his place for lunch, he was entertaining one of his clients. Again ...stupid me. I assumed he'd given them up as well. How could I be so fucking blind?"

"Chad, you had no way of knowing he was going to be like this." Sam led Chad over to the sofa and pulled him down beside him. "After Derek went missing, you became obsessed with him and the few things you knew about him. You placed him way the fuck up on a massive pedestal. He was a really nice guy back then. Gentle, caring, and naïve.

That was the person you've been carrying a torch for all these years. But he no longer exists."

"But I found him. He's right there. I can see him. I can hold him ...I still love him." Chad slumped over, trembling.

"I know, baby. I'm so sorry." Sam quietly stood and went to the kitchen to turn everything off. He came back to the living room to find Chad standing in the middle of the room crying. The image was crushing, the man he loved broken.

He took Chad's hand and led him upstairs into the bedroom.

"I want *my* Derek back," Chad said, letting Sam remove his clothes for him before reluctantly climbing into bed.

"Your Derek is gone, sweetie." Sam lay down on top of the covers and encouraged Chad into his arms.

"He wouldn't be if I'd driven him to work that day."

"You don't know that for sure."

"Fuck, Sam. He's still so damn precious." Chad turned his face into Sam's shoulder and sighed at the comfort of it.

"Chad, I love you ...so much. So please, I'm begging you to stop torturing yourself. If not for your sake, then for mine. I need you in my life. And I need you to be the strong, vibrant man I grew up with. Please, Chad. I need my best friend back."

Chad took Sam's mouth, tasting the familiar warmth, then pulled away, brushing a thumb across Sam's lips.

"When I was in the hospital," he said, "and you fell asleep on my bed. I lay there, listening to you breathing. And I remember thinking it was a sound I could listen to for the rest of my life."

Sam lifted his head.

"You really thought that?" he asked.

"Yeah. That's when I realized I was in love with you."

"Does this mean you're coming back to me?"

Chad nodded.

"It's where I belong, Sam," he replied. "Let's leave the past behind us and move forward."

"Chad, there's nothing I want more than that."

Sam buried his face into Chad's shoulder and cried himself to sleep, clutching desperately to the man he loved. But when Sam awoke, Chad was no longer beside him, and the clothes he'd been wearing were gone.

There was a note on Chad's pillow that simply read, "I'm sorry, Sam. I can't live without him."

Sam sent an email to Chad's dad resigning from his position, and gathered up a few things—the few things that were truly his, and left a note of his own, in case Chad came back to the penthouse, which read, "Please don't try to find me. I lost my best friend and the love of my life today. If you were to seek me out and find me, I wouldn't be the same person you used to know either."

Grasping his engagement ring, Sam pulled it off, kissed it, and set it down next to the note.

Chapter Twenty Three | Saturday

Chad had been walking around since well before midnight. He wasn't convinced he'd done the right thing by leaving Sam and needed to clear his head before moving ahead with Derek.

He arrived at Derek's apartment and knocked lightly on the door. It was three in the morning, and he wasn't expecting Derek to answer, so he pulled out the key Derek had given him and let himself in, quietly turning on one of the small lights inside the door.

As he moved through the room, he almost tripped over an abandoned pair of shoes. They were expensive men's loafers, not at all the kind Derek would wear.

He took a deep breath and scrubbed the tears away from his face as he entered Derek's bedroom. His knees nearly buckled as he confirmed Derek wasn't alone.

Derek listened to Chad entering the bedroom, but stayed silent and pretended to be asleep. He squeezed his eyes shut tightly, praying Chad would just leave.

"Derek?" Chad crouched down at the side of the bed and brushed his hand along Derek's cheek.

"What are you doing here?" Derek whispered. "You're going to wake Spencer up." He looked over his shoulder and lowered his voice even more. "Chad, it's over between us. You have to leave."

"But we love each other."

"I don't, Chad. I'm sorry, but I don't love you. I thought I did, but it was a mistake." With the final lie told, Derek rolled over and closed his eyes.

He almost gave himself away when Chad leaned over and kissed his head, whispering one last time that he loved him …and that he would love him forever.

The pain ripped through his body as Chad left the room and walked out of his life. His plan to drive Chad away had taken every ounce of love he'd carried for Chad for all those years.

There was nothing left, not even for himself.

He started to cry and curled himself into a ball, his body shaking with grief.

"Did you do it?" Spencer asked as he rolled toward Derek and set his hand affectionately on Derek's shoulder.

"Yeah, Spence, he's gone."

"I'm so sorry it didn't work out for the two of you."

Spencer climbed out of bed and put his shirt back on. It had only been necessary for it to look as though he had no clothes on.

"I'm going to go," he said as he stood at the door and looked back at Derek. "Try to take it easy. Call me if you need to talk."

"Thanks, but I'll be fine."

Derek waited until he heard the apartment door close. He opened the drawer of his bedside table and gripped the cold steel steady in his delicate hands—ready.

So ready.

And pressed it to his temple.

Chapter Twenty Four | Sunday

The police cars started arriving shortly after noon. Protocol dictated that the interested parties had to wait for twenty-four hours before filing a missing persons report, but the department had waived the waiting period as a special favor to Carl Parker. He'd contacted them just after eleven-thirty in the morning to report that his son hadn't shown up for a family breakfast.

After a few calls were made, Chad's car was located a few blocks away from the penthouse, but there was no trace of Chad.

The police collected up a few photos they found in Chad's penthouse. They eventually left just after four in the afternoon with little advice, except to phone the police if anyone heard from him.

Chapter Twenty Five | Twenty Years Later

Eddie, a high school senior, was trying to stay focused on the training exercise, but the heat was getting to him. A last minute practice had been announced before the end of last class over the school's loudspeakers, causing more than a few of the football players to groan with exasperation. Their team had made it all the way to the finals, and they were easily the best team in the league, but their coach, Mr. Sheridan, wasn't leaving anything to chance. He had a reputation for winning the Gold Cup each year for their school, and he wasn't going to let this be the year they lost.

"Mr. Sheridan! This is absolute torture," he whined.

"What was that, Edwina?" Mr. Sheridan shouted as he tossed his clipboard down on the ground and stormed across the field. "If you keep whining like a fucking girl, I'm going to buy you a skirt and sign you up for the cheerleading squad."

The rest of the team erupted in a cascade of snorts and howls.

"And that goes for the rest of you as well!"

Mr. Sheridan blew his whistle to start the exercise again. As he headed back to the sidelines of the field, he looked up toward the bleachers, noting Lance had stopped by to watch the end of practice. He redirected his attention back to the boys and ran them through the exercise twice more before letting them run off to the showers. Once they were safely in the change room, he jogged back to where Lance was standing.

Lance crossed his arms and laughed, shaking his head. "You're going to kill those boys."

"They're tough. They can take it."

Mr. Sheridan checked over his shoulder to make sure none of the boys had returned to the field before pulling Lance into his arms. He lay a gentle kiss on Lance's lips and breathed in the intoxicating scent of his cologne.

"They're also lucky to have a coach that cares as much as you do." Lance gazed down at him and grinned. "I was impressed at the staff meeting today when I heard how many of your boys received football scholarships for college."

"They've earned it. But speaking of tough ...how did your poor students fare on that sadistic history final of yours?"

"As usual, I've got a few brilliant stars." Lance stepped back when he heard the sound of a few boys erupting from the change rooms. "More than a few absolute wastes of space. And the rest fall solidly in the nondescript."

"That sounds infinitely better than my business students." Mr. Sheridan headed off across the field, picking up the plastic cones he'd set out on the field for practice, and stacked them in the storage locker with Lance's assistance.

"I don't know why some of them even bother. They'll be lucky to get into community college with their slack-ass attitude toward economics and finance."

"Now, Mister Sam Sheridan …not everyone is destined for an *Ivy League* education like yours."

Sam threw the storage locker door closed, locked it up, and turned back to face Lance. "I know. I just wish they'd try a little harder." He pocketed the keys.

Lance shoulder checked Sam playfully as they headed toward the parking lot. "Hey, are we still on for dinner tonight?"

"I might have to postpone." Sam opened his car door and leaned on the roof. "I'm meeting with a new student and his parents later on tonight." He scrubbed his hand wearily across his face and sighed. "From everything I've read about him, I may be looking at my next star player."

Lance watched Sam's sinking posture, confused by his lack of enthusiasm. "You should be elated." He set his hand on Sam's back and tried to make eye contact. "What's up?"

"It's nothing." Sam stood up straighter and tried to appear more animated. "He's a Canadian kid. He's moved down here from a school very close to where I grew up." He smiled at Lance. "It just brings back a lot of memories. Ones I'd rather forget."

"Tell you what? Rather than going to some crowded restaurant, I'll cook for you at my place. And then I can attempt to unwind all this stress you're carrying …in private."

"I might not be the best company tonight."

"Nonsense. You wouldn't have to say a word." Lance grinned as Sam let a shy smile slip across his face. "So, is that a *yes*?"

"Yes, that's a *yes*."

Sam slid into the driver's seat of his car, slammed the door shut, and tried to roll the window down to speak to Lance, but it was sticking, as usual, so he opened the door again.

"When are you going to get rid of this piece of crap?" Lance tapped loudly on the top of the car.

"When they start paying high school teachers a decent wage."

"That's not what I meant."

"Hey, I happen to like this piece of crap. It has spirit."

"That would imply it is indeed dead, or at the very least, on its last legs, and I would have to agree." Lance leaned closer to Sam and continued tapping lightly on the roof. "I don't understand why you have to be so stubborn."

"We're not talking about this."

"It's just a car."

"Have you seen any of the cars? They're not just cars."

Lance shook his head.

"Which is why I'm all the more mystified," he said. "And besides ...to him ...it's just a car."

"Yes, but you don't understand how he works. First, it's a car. Then it's a house. Then it's an entire, tropical, fucking island. And on and on it would go." He turned the engine over and revved it up. "I refuse to be bought. I'm not ever going back to work for him. I like my life here."

"I'm sorry. I know you're doing what's best for you."

"Thank you." Sam brought his hand to rest on Lance's hip and squeezed it lightly. "I'll try to wrap up the meeting as quickly as possible." He stroked his hand along Lance's leg, pressing his thumb into the crease of Lance's groin. "I'm looking forward to watching you work in the kitchen."

"Be kind. I'm not an accomplished cook like you. Dinner might not be up to your standards."

"Not to worry. I'm more interested in dessert anyway." Sam winked at Lance and let him close the door.

The fluorescent office lights flickered noisily to life, reminding Sam that his life consisted of working in the depths of a smelly, windowless basement of a school, rather than the lofty, airy and sophisticated office he had once held, although briefly.

He dropped into his chair and pulled out the file on the student he'd be meeting tonight, and felt his chest tighten. The irony of a student from Vancouver finding his way down to a school in Arizona was odd enough, but the fact that the student's name was Chad, was almost too much to comprehend. If it weren't for the fact the photo of the boy looked nothing like his first love, he would've had significant trouble using the name.

"Excuse me, Mr. Sheridan?"

Sam looked up and smiled. "Come on in, Chad." He motioned toward a chair and waited for the boy to take a seat. He kept his eyes focused on the door for a second. "Are your parents coming?"

"My dad is parking the car. We were running a bit late, so he sent me in ahead. I hope that's all right."

"That's no problem. We can talk while we wait for him." Sam smiled to put the boy at ease, although he seemed quite confident. "So, tell me. How long have you been playing ball?"

"Since I was nine. My dads thought it would be a good way for me to burn off some energy." Chad grinned and relaxed a little. The coach's eyes had only popped open slightly when he'd mentioned that he had *dads*, plural.

"My parents thought the same thing. I was a bit of a terror around the house."

"Yeah, me too." Chad sighed and laughed. "I was forever being told I was living up to my name."

Sam's face dropped. "What do you mean by that?"

"I was named after a friend of my dad's. Apparently, he was quite the handful as well." Chad smiled shyly. The coach had taken on a blank expression that he found concerning.

"Are you all right?" he asked.

Sam flipped open the folder on his desk and read through the registration forms. Chad's last name was listed as *Sugar*; a name he had no recollection of from high school.

"What is your other dad's name?" Sam asked. "The registration form only lists an *Ashton Spencer Winston* as your guardian."

"He's my adoptive father. He and my dad were partners when I was born. They both raised me."

"So, they decided to use your non-adoptive dad's last name?" Sam leaned forward on his desk. "That's a nice idea, actually."

"No, my dad's last name isn't really *Sugar*."

Sam leaned back in his chair and tried to collect his thoughts. "Then why do you have the last name *Sugar*?"

"I don't know. Some crazy thing about leaving a clue or something. Apparently, my dad was a bit obsessive when it came to naming me. It had to be *Chad Sugar*."

Sam closed his eyes and tried to control the rate at which his heart was accelerating. He remembered now where he'd heard the name *Sugar* before.

"Mr. Sheridan?" Chad said. "Have I said something wrong? Did you know my dad or something?"

Sam looked up when he heard someone walking toward his office. A flash of movement stepped through the doorway and appeared as a ghost before him. By all accounts, the figure now standing in his office was supposed to have died nearly twenty years ago.

His mind went blank as the apparition spoke.

"You're a hard man to find, Sam." Derek smiled as he sat down next to his son. "Now, tell me. Would it be all right if I spoke to Chad Parker? He's even harder to track down than you are."

The waitress filled the men's coffee cups, yet again. She checked her watch and cursed under her breath; she was supposed to have been off twenty minutes ago. She had a hot date tonight, but she didn't know how much longer he was going to wait for her. She could see him pacing around outside the diner, working his way through his tenth cigarette; he was pissed.

"Do you two need anything else?" she asked.

"No, dear, we're fine," Derek said as he crushed out his cigarette. "You don't want to keep that dreamboat of yours waiting." He winked at her and gazed out the window at the sullen, pimply faced teen skulking around outside.

She sneered obstinately at him and headed for the door.

"So, the night you walked out on Chad—" Derek turned his attention back to Sam. "That was the night he went missing?"

"I didn't walk out on him." Sam reached for the sugar packets and stirred two into his cup. "He'd already made his decision."

Derek pulled out another cigarette, but found it difficult to light; his hands were shaking so badly. He finally had it lit and settled back into his seat. "And you have no idea where he is?"

"Fuck, Derek. I don't care where he is. He's not working for his dad anymore, and the last I heard, he'd taken off on some damn world tour or something. He's completely off the grid most of the time." Sam leaned on the table and pulled out his wallet and a pen. "Look, this is Evelyn's number." He quickly scrawled a phone number on the back of an old receipt. "She won't tell you where Chad is, but she might be persuaded to get a message to him."

"Thanks, but she won't take my calls. I've tried. Her secretary is convinced I'm some kind of psychopath intent on destroying Evelyn's son." Derek blew the smoke away from Sam and butted out his cigarette. "When was the last time you spoke to him?"

Sam drained his coffee, preparing to leave.

"He used to call me sometimes," he answered. "But I kept hanging up on him. At some point in the conversation, he always ended up mentioning you. I couldn't take it. Eventually, he got the message. He doesn't call anymore."

Sam settled back in.

"That night," he said, lowering his voice. "Chad ran back into your apartment building when he heard the emergency vehicles. Your apartment manager told him you'd killed yourself. Shot yourself in the head." He sighed deeply. "He went missing …for months. When we found him …he was a mess, barely holding on, intent on following you."

Derek just stared out the window. He'd known. Known Chad wouldn't go quietly. That he wouldn't go back to Sam. He'd hoped—prayed.

But suicidal?

Sam touched Derek's arm.

"Derek, before I go, I have to ask you one question. What the fuck really happened that night?"

Lance kissed the back of Sam's neck and lowered himself onto the bed beside him. He rolled over and turned the bedside light off before encouraging Sam into his arms. The room was as silent as it had been throughout their entire lovemaking; Sam was utterly distracted.

"Penny for your thoughts?" Lance asked.

"I'm sorry. It's not every day you see a ghost."

"Especially a ghost as hot as that. I can see why you were distracted. When I came to pick you up from that diner tonight, I have to admit, a streak of jealousy ran through my veins."

Sam yawned and tucked himself against Lance's side. "Don't be ridiculous. Derek is just ...well, Derek."

"That doesn't give me much to go on." Lance grinned and kissed the top of Sam's head. "Where did you say you knew him from?"

"He went to Tekla."

"Mm ...well. Derek obviously wasn't a football player like you. Not with that lithe and seductive little body of his." Lance pulled Sam closer to him and tucked his face up next to his ear. "Please tell me you did him in high school."

Sam's anger exploded as he threw the covers back, and stormed off into the washroom, slamming the door, and leaving Lance chastising himself for misreading the situation.

"Sam, I'm sorry." Lance climbed out of bed, approached the bathroom door, and knocked lightly. "I'm an ass. I know. I'm sorry." He let himself sink onto the floor and leaned his head against the door. "Let's start this again." He waited, but there was no response. "Why did you think Derek was dead?"

Sam wrapped his hands over his head as he sat on the toilet and tried to calm himself. He really didn't want to get into this with Lance. He reached over and pulled a ream of toilet tissue off the roll, and dabbed lightly at his nose.

"Sam? Please, you can talk to me. What's going on?" Lance sighed when he didn't receive a response and made to stand up.

"He shot himself in the head," Sam said. "That's the last I heard. That he killed himself."

Lance tucked himself up and prepared to listen. It was a rare thing for Sam to open up to him, and he didn't want to ruin it by interrupting, so he kept quiet.

"He said the gun jammed," Sam said. "When he finally got a shot off, he only grazed his head ...his hands were shaking so bad."

"So, he really was trying to kill himself."

"Yeah." Sam shook his head in sympathy. "He was in a lot of pain ...he wanted to end it. He was reloading the gun when a john of his ran back into his apartment. He'd heard the first shot."

"His client?" Lance grinned. "That dish was a fucking hustler?"

Silence.

"Sam? I'm sorry ...I didn't mean to—"

"It's all right. His partner, Spencer, was the john that stopped him from ending it that night. That was their kid I met tonight."

"Wow. That's a bizarre coincidence."

"It was no coincidence. Derek was looking for me."

"Why?"

"He's looking for the man he named his son after, and he assumed I would know where to find him." Sam paused and ran his hand aggressively through his hair. "He's still in love with him."

"Who is it?" Lance leaned closer to the door, curious as to what the answer might be. "What's the kid's name?" He fell forward as the bathroom door was pulled open.

Sam emerged, stepped over Lance and wandered over to the bed, and flopped down onto it. "The kid's name is Chad."

"Get the fuck out!" Lance laughed and clambered to his feet, throwing himself on the bed beside Sam. "The nut job that keeps sending you cars? That hot little number is in love with that lunatic? I guess there really is no accounting for taste."

Sam grew quiet, and Lance sighed as he realized he'd fucked up, yet again. "Jeez, Sam. I'm sorry."

"Can I stay here tonight?" Sam climbed further up the bed and tucked a pillow under his head. "I don't feel like going home."

"Sure. I'll drop you off at your car in the morning. We don't want to arrive at school together."

"Fucking unbelievable."

Sam grabbed one of the other pillows and buried his face in it, making Lance cringe when he started screaming into it.

"What the hell did I say this time?" Lance asked.

"It's not you. It's Derek and his fucking legacy!" Sam shouted as he threw the pillow off. "It always has to come back to him. Always! Always! Always!"

"What the hell are you on about?"

"Chad was obsessed with Derek. We had to arrive at Grad as a couple, holding hands so everyone would see we were together. That we were a couple." Sam sat up suddenly, causing Lance to lurch back in surprise. "Chad had only known Derek for a week. We'd been best friends since we were eight years old."

"Who? Who was your best friend? Derek?"

"No. Chad." Sam crashed back down on the bed and closed his eyes. "God, I loved him." He opened his eyes and looked at Lance, hoping for understanding. "But he never stopped loving Derek. Even after we were engaged to be married."

"You were engaged? To Chad?"

"We were together for seven years."

"Fuck, Sam. Why didn't you tell me who Chad really was?"

"It was too painful. I wanted to forget."

"But you were engaged to him. He was obviously an important person in your life, and you led me to believe he was just some rich nutjob trying to hire you back into his company."

"I'm sorry, but it wasn't something I ever wanted to talk about again. Chad never loved me the way he loved Derek. The only reason he's chasing after me now, and sending me stuff, is because he thinks Derek is dead."

"Jeez, that's fucked up." Lance lay down beside Sam and stroked some of the hair from Sam's eyes, lingering to stroke his eyebrows. "Are you still in love with him?"

"Don't," Sam replied. "I don't want to talk about him anymore."

Lance rolled onto his back and stared up at the ceiling.

"Hey, I'm sorry," Sam said.

"I'm just trying to be supportive."

"I know you are. I'm sorry."

"Is Chad the reason you totally shut me out whenever I try to get closer to you emotionally?" Lance looked back over at Sam and studied his face. "Fuck. What is it with this guy?"

"It doesn't matter. As soon as Chad finds out Derek is alive, nothing else will matter to him." Sam tried to smile, but the tears broke his cover. "He'll leave me alone after that."

"Damn it, Sam. You're still in love with him, aren't you?"

Sam nodded.

"I can't help it," he said.

"Sam, I've dreamed of the day you would finally open up to me about your secret life in the great white north, but I had no idea it was so fucked up." Lance grinned widely and pulled Sam into his arms. "You know I love you, right?"

"Yeah, I know." Sam sighed and studied the sharp line of Lance's jaw. He leaned in closer and kissed it. "I love you, too."

"But it's not the same, is it?"

Sam pushed Lance away, annoyed, and rolled over. "Why do you do this? I said I loved you. Why is that not good enough for you?" He tucked his knees up and listened to Lance breathing tentatively behind him. "He left me a week before our wedding. It broke my heart. I don't think I'll ever fully recover. I love you as much as I'll ever be able to."

"So, he was your best friend and the love of your life. I can't even hope to compete with that." Lance poked at Sam's ribs playfully, making him squirm. "And he's loaded." He kissed the back of Sam's neck and tucked his face in against him. "I haven't got a fucking chance, have I?"

"You have more than a chance."

Lance grinned happily. "So, how rich is he exactly?"

Sam rolled back over, gripped Lance's hands, and smiled mischievously. "Obscenely."

He kissed Lance's chin then began kissing a line down the center of Lance's body with his lips.

"Obscenely. Now, there's a word I like to hear coming from your lips." Lance closed his eyes and gasped in exhilaration as Sam's warm mouth found its target.

The hotel room took on a ghastly hue as Derek turned the last of the lights off. They needed to find a proper house as soon as possible. The thought of spending another night in a hotel, even one as extravagant as this, was beyond repulsive to him. It brought back far too many memories of a life left far behind.

He slipped into the bathroom and carefully closed the door over before turning the light on, not wanting to wake Spencer and their son. He examined his face in the mirror and wondered what Sam had seen in his eyes as they'd spoken. Twenty years ago, he'd been prepared to end his life so Chad could be with Sam, only to have Sam tell him he'd left Chad that very same night.

The revelation had almost brought him to his knees.

Life had been a blur after that night in his apartment. Spencer had taken charge of him, whisking him away and booking him into the best rehabilitation center in the country. He'd spent an entire year there working through the lingering effects of his drug addiction, his life on the streets, and how everything he'd been through with Chad, losing Chad—twice, had contributed to his decision to end his life.

Derek flicked off the light and crept back into the room. He wanted to check on Spencer one last time before he climbed into bed. Approaching Spencer's bedside, he could see Spencer was still awake, waiting for him.

"Hey, Spence," he said as he sat down on the edge of the bed. "You should be asleep by now."

"I wanted to find out how your evening went." Spencer coughed a couple of times and tried to regulate his breathing. "You were so excited to have found Sam. How could I sleep?"

"Easy." Derek laughed softly. "You could start by shutting your eyes." He stroked Spencer's face then bent down and kissed his forehead. "You need your sleep."

"I can sleep when I'm dead."

Derek lowered his head and closed his eyes. "Please stop saying that. I'm not ready to let you go yet."

Spencer shifted his body, moving closer and cringed as his arm became trapped under his body.

"Here. Don't do that," Derek said, gently pushing Spencer's body over enough to release his arm so he could set it on top of the blankets. "I know you hate it when I wrap you up like a *fucking burrito*, but if I don't, you'll flail around all night, lose your blankets, and freeze to death."

"If only it were that easy. I hear one falls asleep all peaceful like when one freezes to death." Spencer frowned when he saw Derek shiver. "I'm sorry. I'll stop." He reached out to hold Derek's hand, gripping it as tightly as he could manage.

"Is Sam going to let you talk to Chad?" he asked.

"He doesn't know where he is. They're not together."

Spencer coughed, spitting, and gripped tighter onto Derek's hand. He eventually managed to get his breathing back under control so he could speak. "I'm so sorry, sugar. What now?"

"Now, we enjoy the warmth of Arizona and try to get some color back in your cheeks. I didn't move us all the way down here strictly for my benefit." Derek glanced over at the bedside table and picked up the greeting card that was propped against the lamp. "Do you want me to read the card from Julie again?"

"She's a wonderful girl, isn't she?"

"She loves her dad, that's for sure. And I can't fault anyone who loves you as much as I do."

Spencer laughed to himself. "We've had it good, haven't we?"

"Yes, we have." Derek smiled. "It's been a wonderful twenty years." He let his mind wander back to the weekend visits Spencer had paid him while he was in the rehabilitation center. They'd become really close as their roles had been reversed, with Spencer listening to Derek's deepest insecurities and hopes for the future. When he'd been released from the center, Spencer had surprised him by asking him to move in and become his life partner.

He dropped his gaze as he felt a tear escaping.

"I wouldn't be here if it weren't for you," he whispered.

"We agreed to move past that." Spencer patted Derek on the leg. "You were always there for me in my darkest hours. I was just returning the favor."

"I don't know what I'm going to do without you."

"You're going to find the love of your life, and you're going to live out the rest of your days wrapped in his arms."

Derek sniffed as the tears coated his face. He wiped them away with his shirtsleeve and turned back to find that Spencer had finally succumbed to the exhaustion of the day. He leaned in and kissed Spencer's lips, noting with sorrow how cold they were. He brushed his fingers across them, and pulled the blankets up, wishing he could climb in and share his body heat.

Those days were over though. Doing so, climbing in, would add to the growing number of bruises on Spencer's already fragile skin.

He gasped silently, realizing just how little time he had left with him.

Chapter Twenty Six | Soon, Very Soon

The phone rang twice before it went to voicemail. Sam jammed his thumb onto the end button and threw the phone across his desk. He watched it skid serenely toward the edge and teeter. It was all Sam could do not to laugh aloud as it buzzed and fell onto the floor. The thought of a suicidal phone played through his mind as he rounded his desk and picked up the scattered pieces required to connect him to the world. As he pushed the last section back into place, the phone came alive and displayed a caller he hadn't spoken to in ages.

"Hey, Evelyn," Sam said as he sat back in his chair.

"Sam, darling. How are you?"

"I'm doing really well."

"Are you stilling coaching that winning football team?"

"Still coaching. Still winning."

"Good for you." Evelyn paused, and Sam waited for her to continue. It wasn't like Evelyn to be at a loss for words.

"Evelyn, is everything all right?"

"I'm not sure. I'm confused, Sam." Evelyn paused again and exhaled lightly. "My secretary transferred a strange call to my private line this morning from a man named Spencer

Winston. Now, I know him by name, because his family has always been very generous with their contributions to my charities over the years, but he says he knows you."

Sam squirmed in his chair. He knew he should've phoned Evelyn himself. He just couldn't bring himself to do it.

"Well, I wouldn't say I know him," he said. "Not very well, anyway." Sam's breath caught, and he closed his eyes. It was time. Time to sacrifice his heart for the man he loved.

"What else did he say?" he asked.

"He was a little difficult to make out. I don't know if you follow the social circles these days, but he's dying of lung cancer. He's in the end stages."

"No …no, I wasn't aware of that."

"Apparently, his partner of twenty years is caring for him on his deathbed." Evelyn sighed. "Sam, if you could've heard him. He told me his partner has rarely left his side since he was diagnosed two years ago. There was so much love in his voice. It was absolutely heartbreaking."

Sam swiped away the tears and covered his mouth, attempting to compose himself. Derek hadn't told him anything about what he was going through with Spencer.

"He asked me to relay a message to you, on his behalf," Evelyn said.

Sam pinched his nose. "Couldn't he have phoned me himself?"

"I asked him that, but he said it was important that your response was relayed back through me to Chad." Evelyn fiddled nervously with the phone, wondering what the puzzle meant.

"What was the message?"

"That's the funny thing. Spencer said you would be the one to ask."

Sam lowered his eyes and turned his chair away from the windows looking out onto the gymnasium. The next class was starting to filter in. "All I ever wanted was his love ..."

Evelyn was silent at the other end.

"That's all he had to do," Sam said. "He just had to love me."

"He does love you, Sam."

"No—" Sam wiped some tears from his face and fiddled with a loose thread hanging from his shirt. "It was never meant to be. It's time for me to let him go."

"I think you're right, Sam. It tore my heart out, what my son did to you. But it brings me some peace to know you're trying to move on." Evelyn stopped to dab lightly at her eyes. "Is that the message Spencer wanted me to give to Chad? That you're moving on."

"No. Tell Chad his cosmic chain is intact, and the other end is looking for him ...he'll understand."

The wind whipping up across the open desert to the west of the field was making it impossible to continue the game. The referee had finally had enough, and he'd called the game before any more players were taken off the field due to the blowing sand.

Derek shielded his eyes and carefully picked his way down off the bleachers and headed toward the sidelines to speak to Sam while his son and the rest of the team rushed into the change rooms. He slowed down when he saw Sam race across the field in the opposite direction and leap into the arms of a man he couldn't make out. It didn't look like Lance from where he was standing, but then he didn't have his glasses with him, so it was hard to tell.

He stopped and crossed his arms and watched the interaction. Something so familiar. He reached for the tree nearest him, his heart reverberating in his throat—the booming sound of the other man's laugh was easily recognizable. His world slowed, becoming sluggish and surreal when Sam turned to face him and pointed in his direction.

Derek took a deep breath and time came rushing back at him in a torrent of color, sound, and speed when the man standing with Sam stumbled, took off, and came streaking toward him.

Lifted into the air and spun around, all Derek could think to do was cry. He tucked his head into Chad's neck and clung desperately to him, not wanting to loosen his grip and find that it was all a dream. He was trembling uncontrollably by the time Chad set him down and took his mouth, melting him into submission.

The other parents in the stands could be heard grumbling about the shameless display of affection, including a few choice slurs, but Derek had never cared less about anything in his life. He was back where he belonged, in Chad's arms, and he was never letting go again.

He clutched tightly to the front of Chad's shirt and tucked his head into the curve of his neck when Chad gasped joyfully and released his mouth.

"Please don't let go of me," Derek said.

"Never again," Chad said as he beamed down at Derek. "Sam said you were here ...alive. But I wouldn't allow myself to truly believe it until I had you in my arms." He stole another kiss and lingered near Derek's lips. "God, you're still so damn precious."

Chad gripped the wine glass carefully in both his hands, not wanting to drop it. His eyes wandered over Derek's delicate features as he tried to come to grips with what Derek was telling him, that he'd deliberately driven him away twenty years ago.

"You did it because you loved me?" Chad said. "I'm sorry, Derek, but that's really fucked up."

"I know that now." Derek took a long draw off his cigarette and leaned forward in his chair.

Chad wrinkled his nose.

"When did you start smoking?"

"Mm, ...that's Spencer's fault. It's insane, I know. He desperately wants me to quit and I will once he's gone." Derek crushed the cigarette out. "But right now, I need the comfort it brings me."

"You really love him, don't you?"

Derek dipped his head to one side and then moved to sit beside Chad on the sofa. "He saved my life. And not just by taking that gun out of my hands. He saw something in me that I didn't."

Chad nodded. "Incredible strength juxtaposed against stunning innocence."

Derek crunched up his face in dismay. "That's unbelievable." He dropped his gaze, shaking his head. "I'm such a fucking idiot."

"The only idiotic thing you did was not trusting me with my own feelings." Chad set his wine glass down and stroked Derek's face. "I wanted to spend my life with you. Not Sam."

"But you and Sam—"

"Fell in love. But there was so much history between us that there were times when I'd look at him and only see the *old* Sam. The one I used to play trucks with and beat up if he ran faster than me at track meets. It didn't feel right. I loved him, and I knew I wanted him in my life, but not like that."

Derek sighed heavily and rested his head on Chad's shoulder, and thought about how different things would've been if he'd run away with Chad twenty years ago rather than driving him away. He checked the time on his phone and pulled himself off the sofa.

"I have to turn Spencer."

"Do you need any help?"

"I can do it myself. I've been taking care of Spencer like this for weeks." Derek grabbed Chad's hand and pulled him toward the bedroom. "But he knows you're here, so he's probably awake. And if I don't bring you in to see him, I'll never hear the end of it."

Sam watched the patterns of light laid out by the passing cars soar across the ceiling in rows of illuminated bubbles. He tried to count how many cars had gone by since Lance had last spoken.

"Lance, this is ridiculous."

"Ridiculous? You have never run into *my* arms like that."

"That's because you don't want anyone to know about us." Sam rolled onto his side and sighed with exasperation. "I hadn't seen him in twenty years. The last time we were together, I'd fallen asleep in his arms thinking he'd come back to me for good."

"You kissed him in front of everyone."

"It wasn't that kind of kiss, and you know it." Sam rolled back and stared at the ceiling again. "Are you upset because I kissed him, or because I kissed him in front of everyone?"

"Both ...Sam, everyone is going to think you're gay. Guys don't kiss each other like that."

"Here's a newsflash for you, Lance ...I am gay!"

Sam pulled himself off the bed, wrapped his shoulders in a blanket, and dropped down into a chair in the corner of the bedroom. "And I hate to break it to you ...but letting me fuck you up the ass the way I just did ...pretty gay!"

"Fuck off!"

Sam struggled out of the blanket and threw it onto the ground as he bolted toward the bed. "No! You, fuck off! I'm tired of running around hiding. We're grown men, and we're supposed to be in love with each other. But instead of that, I feel like a little kid sneaking around, trying not to get caught because I kissed the boy next door."

"You *did* just kiss the boy next door! In front of everyone!"

"Oh, for fuck's sake!" Sam turned away from Lance in exasperation and scoured the floor for his clothes.

Lance rolled to the edge of the bed and hung over it, trying to reach out to Sam. "Where are you going? I thought you were going to stay at my place tonight."

Sam slipped his pants on and tucked the rest of his clothing under his arm. "I don't know. Somebody might see us."

"Stop it. Please don't go." Lance tugged lightly on Sam's pant leg and looked up at him. "I'm sorry."

Sam took Lance's hands in his and kissed them, and watched as Lance's expression softened. "I know you're scared, and I'm not going to suggest that we come out in front of the whole school in some grand gay gesture, but if we love each other as much as we say we do ...then we need to establish ourselves as a couple in this community."

"I know. But let's start small." Lance smiled as an image floated through his head. "I think the *grand gay gesture* prize may have already been awarded to Chad for kissing you and then practically devouring Derek on the sidelines. I thought Chad was going to hop on and fuck Derek right there on the bleachers."

Sam grinned and nestled in beside Lance. "Chad always was a bit unrestrained when it came to boys." He used his thumb to brush Lance's cheek and then kissed him. "The number of times we had to save Chad's ass—"

"We?"

"Yeah. There were five of us growing up." Sam fiddled contentedly with the loose strands of hair over Lance's ears while he let his mind drift back. "Chad, me, and Dillon. Everyone called us the three musketeers. They thought we were inseparable. Turns out they were wrong."

"What about the other two?"

"Augustus and Tyler. Complete stoners, but they were the most loyal friends a guy could ever ask for."

"What happened?"

"Well. Picture this. The final year of high school. Dillon, Tyler, and Gus catch Chad and I making out at his locker."

"They didn't know you were together?"

"They didn't know I was gay."

Lance snorted out a laugh. "Fuck, that's brutal."

"It gets better. Chad, in his infinite wisdom, proceeds to tell them he's been fucking me for months." Sam grinned and kissed Lance. "I think it was that last part that really did it for them. They never spoke to us again."

"You don't seem that upset about it."

Sam shrugged.

"In some ways," he said, "it was worth losing them. Chad and I had an amazing run." Then he laughed and fell back on the pillows, snorting happily.

"That man was an absolute maniac in bed," he added.

"Thanks, I needed to know that."

"No, this is good. I'm reminiscing about something in my past." Sam pulled Lance down onto the bed and climbed on top of him. "I've moved past him. Chad kissed me today, and it was nice, I'll admit, but all I can think about right now is being with you. I want to be with you, not him. I'm in love with *you.*"

Chapter Twenty Seven | Coming Home

Chad interlaced his fingers with Derek's and held him close to his body as he led him to the door that opened up onto the main sitting room of the Winston family home. As the door swung open, he knew he was going to have to step back and hope that Derek would be able to make his own way to the front of the room where he would be sharing a few words about Spencer.

It had been a crushing reality for Derek when Spencer died, and he'd found himself essentially an outsider when it came to planning the funeral. And adding further injury, it had been decided by Spencer's family that Derek and his son would not be permitted to attend the funeral unless they agreed to keep their lifestyle and the nature of their relationship with the deceased to themselves. Derek had immediately fallen into a deep depression, and Chad had spent days trying to get Derek out of bed, only to find him up and fully dressed on the day of the funeral.

"Are you sure you want to do this?" Chad asked.

Derek nodded.

"Then I'll be right here waiting for you." Chad ran his hand down Derek's arm and squeezed his hand.

Chad peered into the room and located his namesake, and motioned for him to join his dad. He stepped back as Derek's son took over, and watched as they made their way up to the front of the room before finding a seat at the back.

Derek cleared his throat and began, and by the time he was finished, there was no doubt in anyone's mind that Spencer had spent his final days being cared for by people that loved him, and that he'd experienced a rare and fortunate thing. He'd found and experienced true love in his life.

His eulogy complete, Derek nodded with satisfaction as Spencer's daughter, Julie, smiled through swaths of tears, tapping her hands together, as though to clap. She winked at him and gave him a big *thumbs up* as he made his way down the aisle.

His heart only began to slow as he collapsed in a seat next to Chad. "I did it," he said.

"That you did," Chad said as an amused smile danced across his face. "I thought you weren't supposed to bring all that up."

"It would've been dishonest and disrespectful of me to veil a beautiful relationship between two people that lasted two decades and never once faltered." Derek stroked the crease in his pants. "And brought to fruition an intelligent and caring person like our son. Spencer and I loved each other. People need to know that."

"You're absolutely right." Chad rubbed Derek's leg with the back of his hand. "And I'm proud of you."

"I want to thank you, Chad. You've been wonderful through all this." Derek reached down and gripped Chad's hand. "I know this wasn't what you were expecting when you found me, but I'll get there. I'm just going to need some time to heal." He squeezed Chad's hand tighter. "Please know I still want to be with you. And that I still love you as madly as I ever did."

Chad studied Derek's eyes, marveling at the love radiating toward him. "You take as much time as you need. But I'll have you know, Spencer made me promise I'd never let you go again. So don't be thinking I'm going to let you go through this alone."

Derek laughed, exhausted.

"Right now I just want to go home," he said.

"Sure, we'll find Chad, and then I'll have you back at your place in a few minutes."

"No," Derek said. "As soon as I'm done here, in Arizona, I want you to take me *home*. I'll never forget my life with Spencer, but I need to make a fresh start with you …in the place we should have begun our lives together."

Derek looked around the room and tried to figure out what changes had been made. The furniture placement was similar to what he remembered, and he was pleased to see Evelyn had abandoned the light colored carpets. He tucked his arms around his body protectively as he wandered over to the L-shaped sofa, and then ran his hand along the back of it. Chad had insisted it be pulled out of storage and reupholstered for his homecoming. He carefully stepped up onto the edge and made his way into the back corner where Chad had first held him, and where Chad had spent two months of his life waiting for him. He sank down into the cushions and let the emotions wash over him.

"I was planning on never leaving this spot," Chad said as he climbed in behind Derek and wrapped him up in his arms. "I had all the pictures, and stuff from your bedroom set out on the coffee table behind me so I could reach everything." He closed his eyes and nestled his face in the soft curls of Derek's hair.

"It's surreal being back here," Derek said as he pushed his body deeper into Chad's arms. "When I asked you to take me home, I had no idea we were actually going to move back in with your parents."

"I don't think my parents were expecting it either. But it really is where our lives together should've begun."

Derek smiled. "And I have never heard Chad sound so excited. I told him it was like teen heaven in here, but he didn't believe me." He dropped his head back and looked up at Chad. "Where is my son, anyway?"

"My mom took him shopping …for clothes."

Derek turned and glared at him. "What?"

"I'm sorry. I know how much Chad hates it, and I tried to convince my mom to do something else with him, but I had my own selfish reasons for wanting him out of the house for your homecoming today …so, I caved to her demands."

"That poor child. He'll be scarred for life."

"I'm sure he'll survive. My mom adores him."

"It sounds like he's adjusted all right. Even without me here."

"He's a smart kid. He understood why you needed to be alone while you put Spencer's affairs in order."

"I'm sorry it took so long."

"Hey, a few weeks of waiting is nothing to complain about when we have the rest of our lives together." Chad kissed the top of Derek's head and breathed in the scent of him.

"So your selfish reasons for sending my son into his own private hell. What would those be?"

"Well," Chad said as he stood up and helped Derek off the sofa. "Seeing as I haven't held you properly in over twenty years, I thought we could lock ourselves in the bedroom for the rest of the day and catch up on lost time."

"Mm …keep talking. I may just drop the child abuse charges."

Derek followed Chad into the small sitting room located just inside Chad's suite. His eyes wandered over the items set out on the tables and bookcases, and his breath caught as he recognized the many cherished objects he'd packed up from his childhood bedroom so many years ago.

"You kept everything?" Derek said as he let his fingers drift along the smooth frame surrounding his first baby photo.

"I couldn't part with any of it, so I packed everything away in storage." Chad stepped up behind Derek and set his hands on his shoulders. "I had some of the girls unpack everything last week. Chad had an absolute riot going through your photo album."

"I bet he did." Derek turned to face Chad and wrapped his arms around Chad's body, burying his face in Chad's chest.

"Hey, what's wrong?"

"Nothing is wrong. Everything is perfect." Derek kissed Chad's chest and looked up into his face. "I love you so much."

"Hold that thought. I have something I want to show you."

Derek followed Chad to the door leading into the bedroom and waited while Chad appeared to be collecting himself.

"The night you went missing," Chad said finally. "I'd done up my room for you. So your first time would be special."

"You didn't—"

"I did. I knew how important it was to you, and I wanted to show you how much I respected that." Chad unlatched the door and pushed it open, letting Derek enter before him. "I think it's pretty close to how it was that night."

Derek stepped into the room, overwhelmed by the sheer quantity of rose petals and lit candles scattered throughout the space. He lowered himself down onto the bed and gathered up a handful of petals to hold to his face.

"It's beautiful, Chad," he said and motioned for Chad to join him on the bed. As the weight of Chad's body lowered onto his, Derek was infused with a profound sense of peace.

And as he wrapped his arms around Chad's body and felt the warm touch of Chad's breath on his neck, he knew for sure they'd been destined for one another, and that after all these years, he'd come home at last.

About the Author

Leigh Jarrett is a queer, quirky, and passionate author of LGBTQ Romantic Fiction. Lover of antique stores, the smell of lye and oil as it turns to soap, and the awe-inspiring majesty of the ancient Douglas firs of Vancouver Island's Cathedral Grove.

In her hometown of Kelowna, BC, Leigh can be found nestled up with her fabulously supportive wife, her trusty laptop, and their persistent treat seeker, Miss Mimi-dog.

Please consider joining Leigh's mailing list:
http://eepurl.com/xuhej

To connect with Leigh Jarrett:
Email: leigh@leighjarrett.com
Website: www.leighjarrett.com
You can also find Leigh on Facebook and Twitter

THE STARS ON MY ARM

TEKLA SERIES

Joel Carrigan and his girlfriend, Erica, are excited about starting their graduating year at Tekla Senior High. The long hot summer is drawing to a close, and their plans for a promising future together are on track. But their carefully laid plans are about to be disrupted by a dark and seductive force neither one of them anticipated.

That force is named Ethan Cooke. His gothic persona, covered in tattoos, piercings, and reckless abandon, set Joel's heart racing—but not out of fear.

SIMPLY MARVELLOUS

TEKLA SERIES

Annie Luka has always been home-schooled, but she's convinced her mother to let her attend public school for her graduating year. When it is learned that Annie Luka is actually Attila Luka, a beautiful cross-gender guy struggling with his identity, it tears a small group of friends apart. Only when they all reunite years later is the full extent of Attila's deception revealed, bringing some of the group closer together, and pushing others further apart.

What transpires over the next few years after the reunion leaves Attila wondering if he'll ever find true love.

Other Books by Leigh Jarrett

<u>Drakkar Coven Series</u>

Callum of Drakkar Coven

Oleander, Son of Drakkar

Alexander, Prince of the North (Coming soon!)

Shadows On My Soul

Possession Pointe

Healing Hands of E'lan